# Travels with Old Befana

Donna Kendall

Travels with Old Befana
Donna Kendall

ISBN-13: 978-1499615371
ISBN-10: 149961537X

Library of Congress Number: applied for

Primary category: Fiction – adult and young adult. General

Country of Publication: United States

Publication date: October, 2014

Language: English

Italian legends, Christmas legends, Folk Tales, Faith, Romance, Friendship, Christian Cultural traditions

## About the Author

Donna Kendall is the author of fiction novels: *Sailing on an Ocean of Tears* and *In the Shadows of Sins*. She has also published a biographical memoir, *Dancing with Bianchina*, and two children's stories: *Stitch-A-Story*, and *Uncle Charlie's Soup*. *The Consistent Choice: For Better Living in a Better World* was her first non-fiction work. A short story, *A Heart in Bloom* was published in an anthology: *The Story that Must be Told: True Stories of Transformation;* it was autobiographical. She currently writes for the DC Examiner, teaches a variety of courses, and lives in Williamsburg, Virginia.

# Acknowledgements

I am a first generation Italian-American. My parents were born in Cassano, Italy, so, as I child I grew up with the Old Befana legend. My parents, Angelo and Julia, brought Italy into our warm and loving home in Akron, Ohio. I only knew I was in America when I stepped outside the door. On the morning of January 6, the Feast of the Epiphany - the day when the Magi honored the birth of Jesus - I would wake up to some treats in my shoes because Old Befana is the post-Christmas surprise. Christmas was a very special and holy celebration in our home. But, as with any celebration for children, the joys are derived from the gestures of love and the legend of Old Befana meant some extra surprises when the Christmas season was finished. Mind you, as a young child *any* special surprise was welcome at any time. But, let's face it, Santa Claus brings toys, so his presence is more enduring as his gifts are more permanent. Once my Befana cookies were eaten that was it, I'd have to wait another year to get those special treats.

For many years my parents would take my brother Rocco and I to Italy to visit our grandmother, aunts, uncles, cousins, etc... The last time we went as a family my brother was 14, I was 16. I loved going to Italy, to visit family and to visit our native country's enduring beauty. After many years, and as Rocco neared a milestone birthday, he sent me an email saying that he would like to go with me to Italy. I booked the tickets the same day. It was just the two of us and it was a wonderful experience.
It often happens when one visits Italy that people will come to you and say, "When you go to Italy can you bring me back a...." whatever it happens to be, Limoncello, pasta, something innately *Italian*. On this occasion the wife of my brother's friend, Vicki, asked us to bring back a statue of Old Befana. It is mostly Italian-American women who like to keep this statue somewhere in their kitchen to remind them of their heritage. Women in Italy do not need this reminder. As it turned out my brother and I looked in every shop we came across from Rome to Bari and other assorted villages and did not find a statue of Old Befana.

On our return home I was disappointed that we had not been able to bring Vicki her Old Befana statue and it suddenly occurred to me that I had two. Many years ago (probably during other trips to Italy) I came across Old Befana statues, so I purchased two – one for myself and one for my mother. After my mother passed away I had her statue once again. I decided to give Vicki my statue and keep my mother's for myself. My little Befana statue sat on the shelf but for some reason my thoughts kept going to her – why was it so difficult to find her in Italy? What was it about her that marked her as a coveted treasure? I took her off the shelf and put her on my desk because I could not stop thinking of her. As I stared at her I realized she must have a story of her own. Because of her "legend" she has travelled the world, met people, and experienced all kinds of adventures – what does she have to say?

Old Befana's story is about one woman's search for meaning. She travels the world seeking the newborn baby Jesus whom she learned about from the Magi. She continues to search for him until this day. The legend never says that she arrived late in Bethlehem and said *darn, I'm too late; they've already left for Egypt,* then returned home and picked up her life where she left off. According to the legend, she never gives up looking for him. As with us, the more we search for Christ the more we feel a stronger desire to search more deeply. It's tempting to become complacent and say, *I found him a long time ago. I went to Catholic school, I go to church and try to be good.* The search for Christ is never complete. To seek him is to grow in our desire to find him.

Ironically, it was a search for Old Befana that led me to telling this story, *her* story of her search for Christ. She sits on my desk now and serves as a reminder to always seek him in what I do and to carry him with me at all times.

*For my husband, Jim-*
*And for the next generation of little cousins- in Italy, Ohio*
*and around the world - wherever the search for*
*Jesus takes you.*

*Travels with Old Befana*


*By*


*Donna Kendall*

*"I've caught belief like a disease. I've fallen into belief like I fell in love."*
*Graham Greene*

# Prologue

*The Magi Visit the Messiah*

"After Jesus was born in Bethlehem in Judea, during the time of King
Herod, Magi from the east came to Jerusalem and asked, 'Where is the one
who has been born king of the Jews? We saw his star when it rose and have
come to worship him.'
When King Herod heard this he was disturbed, and all Jerusalem with him.
When he had called together all the people's chief priests and teachers of the
law, he asked them where the Messiah was to be born. 'In Bethlehem in
Judea,' they replied, 'for this is what the prophet has written:
'But you, Bethlehem, in the land of Judah,
   are by no means least among the rulers of Judah;
for out of you will come a ruler
   who will shepherd my people Israel.'
Then Herod called the Magi secretly and found out from them the exact
time the star had appeared. He sent them to Bethlehem and said, 'Go and
search carefully for the child. As soon as you find him, report to me, so that
I too may go and worship him.
After they had heard the king, they went on their way, and the star they
had seen when it rose went ahead of them until it stopped over the place
where the child was. When they saw the star, they were overjoyed. On
coming to the house, they saw the child with his mother Mary, and they
bowed down and worshiped him. Then they opened their treasures and
presented him with gifts of gold, frankincense and myrrh. And having been
warned in a dream not to go back to Herod, they returned to their country
by another route."
(Matthew 2:1-12)

# 1

## *Just Call Me Old Befana*

This icy weather in... where am I... Ohio? is just not good for me. This humidity makes the memory of my bursitis flare up. These old bones just don't adapt like they used to. I've travelled around the world for longer than I can remember, from hot arid climates to some really cold hovels and it's never really bothered me, but lately I think I'm starting to feel my age and maybe a bit worn out. The weather here in winter is very pretty but only if I can sit inside where it's warm and look at it through a window. I like seeing where I am now. It's a healthy thing to look out of a new window once in a while.

Travelling around is not a problem so much as my state of mind at any given place. I'm not necessarily happier when everything around me is going well because I can still be downright grumpy and truth-be-told I seem to be quite capable of being chipper when things take a downhill turn. I think the problem sometimes is the unexpected weariness that coils around my heart, or my brain, I'm not sure which, that makes me feel a little testy whether I'm happy or sad. Weariness often comes from carrying around unnecessary memories. Good memories don't weigh anything. But memory can be tricky; I can't remember what I was thinking about two minutes ago but I can remember bygone days and the people that long ago passed through my life and enriched it in one way or another. The past and present seem the same to me. The future is the only thing that's different because I can't see it. A thousand years from now it won't matter what I did today unless it was rooted in love because love is the only thing that lasts and moves the world forward; evil gets thwarted eventually; I've seen that. I've been around long enough to know that history looks at the good things that happen as the bright spots of humanity and scorns our mistakes as *lessons* about what to avoid. If you get to live to a well-seasoned age you're able to see the spectrum of love play out - and win out. Me? I'm in a state of perpetual old age and that has many more blessings, really, than curses. I think what I like best about being "old" is the opportunity it gives me to be present in life instead of dashing through it. You'll forgive me when I go on and on to explain what I've learned along the way; I'm still trying to understand it myself.

I confess that even though every time I turn around I feel like taking a nap, I try to stay vigilant – I don't want to miss a thing. I once lived through self-imposed fog and I don't want to be like that again. It's really a mission of love to pay attention to each moment, to focus on the people in my life at this time, to remember them, even if I can't remember my own name. Which I can't. It's been much too long since anyone has called me by the name I had as a child. What I go by now is more of a title than a name and this title means I'm old and well past my prime. So, I don't look like Sophia Loren – let's face it, I didn't look like her when I was young, either. She was blessed with the looks of feminine perfection and she's been able to carry those blessings into her doting old age. I was blessed with other things, things I could never find in a looking glass, and things which I didn't acquire until I was well past the peak of femininity. My blessings have more to do with a talent for providing something. Oh, maybe it's not really a talent at all; maybe it's just an urge. Travelling far and wide as I have, I've always come across some *thing* or some *one* in need of attention. I guess the talent is in being able to see it. Not far from an abandoned building you'll find an abandoned heart; there are empty places and empty lives; there are broken dreams and broken families; there are hollow ambitions and empty stomachs; the worst is when I find vacant hopes and people adrift. My urge, then, is to help fill the heart, the mind, the tummy, or the void with the love, the thought, the nourishment or the blessing that it takes to inflame that momentary "ahhh" in life, the one that defeats the fear that there is *nothing*.

I'll never forget Aggie at ninety-eight years old lying upon her deathbed, having outlived everyone she loved and bereft of all her things; she was about to make the great leap. I was sitting at her bedside next to potted violets and a box of tissues when she turned to me and said, "I still don't believe there is anything out there." I chuckled and said to her, "Really Aggie? You're smarter than that. I'm here, aren't I? If there is nothing out there then there would be nothing here either." She smiled, then, nodded, and took the big leap.

This is my job. I somehow get from one place to another and I end up in the place where I need to be and maybe to say what someone needs to hear. I am Old Befana – a redundant title if you ask me since there are no young *befanas* that I'm aware of, and since *befana* actually means you've outlived youth and beauty, it's rather indelicate to repeat it. I seem to get around somehow; I move from one part of the world to another. How I came to be here in this place is a rather long tale indeed. The best part of my existence is that no matter where I am I'm always in a place where I'm needed. Wherever I am, I am home.

## 2

### *Old Befana and the Old Days*

Love is a lot like a running stream, it has to find a place to go, to keep moving. It's never meant to stay in one place or be contained. Sure, sometimes it hits some rocks and logs but it must find a way to flow. Love takes you on a journey to places you've never dreamed of. I should know.

I can't tell you how "old" I was at the time, but since I've somehow been immortalized at whatever point this adventure began, I was already called *La Befana* by the locals. I lived in a small village in the southern part of Italy the name of which I can't recall but I do remember how it smelled! It makes me laugh just to think about it. My house was part of a small cluster of huts at the center of town; it was only one room but it was mine. The hard clay floor and the four stone walls were no different than any other house in that little cluster, but my house was always warm because of my two little windows – one faced south and the other east. Also, I had a nice little fireplace for heat and for cooking, a small wooden table and chairs, and a bed made of feathers and hay in the corner near the window that faced east. The sun would wake me up each morning with its insistent rays, like spears shooting into my pillow. I liked that. I also liked the pithy smell of our village that was steeped in mainly compost – manure, merda– whatever you want to call it, there it is, that's the smell I remember, the one that makes me smile. Mind you, it wasn't a bad smell – it was just very *natural*.

Back in those days most of the bigger houses had an attached stable for livestock: goats, chickens, rabbits, cows, what-have-you; people and animals lived rather *strettamente*. People lived side-by-side (literally) with nature. Go ahead and scoff. People nowadays may be convinced that they are more civilized because they live with dogs, cats, and ferrets in the house (even sleeping in their beds) but you know when you're in a house that is shared with pets; it's the special scent that gives it away. The scent of my village had a certain character as well. Each family had its own little garden for vegetables, and the livestock provided dairy products, eggs, or on special occasions, meats. But, the by-products of animals had a distinct purpose; it was needed for compost to fertilize the vegetable gardens. You must understand – you can only use manure from animals that eat vegetation to fertilize plants because this manure carries vegetable nutrients into the soil. If you try to use manure from carnivorous animals there's something nasty in the manure that will actually kill the plants, and *that* manure has an unpleasant smell. We learned this back then. We mixed the good stuff from goats, cows, or sheep manure with decaying vegetables (potato peels, overripe fruit, etc...) to make the richest fertilizer. And so, my village smelled like animals and the carefully-sprinkled compost in our nice little gardens. I've always believed it's ironic that decay and death should provide such an abundance of fertility and life.

The people in my village were excellent gardeners. I was not. The only thing I seemed to be able to grow well was hot peppers. At harvest time, I had enough pepperoncini to supply all of Hell for their infernal parties. My little home was decorated with strands upon strands of peppers hanging up to dry. People in my village never visited – it meant watery eyes to enter my home. But if someone wanted a few pepperoncini to spice up the *pasta diablo*, they'd wait outside near the road until I came out with some peppers and traded them for a sack of flour and sugar.

I lived alone and people generally regarded me as a bit of a kook. I didn't discourage them because I felt they were right for the most part and I didn't care much for them and their habits either. Sticking my rustic nose in the normal rhythms of the village was not for me. Without the flair for conversation I didn't need to sit outside in the evenings and carry the local gossip. It mattered little to me that Margharita was carrying on with Lorenzo in the back of Peppe's horse stall. It didn't concern me that Cici had one leg longer than the other because a donkey had kicked his mother Lucrezia in the belly while she was pregnant. What did it matter to me that crazy Luigi talked to the olive trees and that they talked to him? They once told him he would find a little sack of gold beneath a rock in the grotto outside of town. He spent a week looking under every rock he could find in and out of the grotto. Finally, after bringing a trowel with him he found an old signet ring engraved with a big "R" on the face. It probably belonged to Reggio Ricardo the signore of this village before it was pillaged by the Sicilians from that island off the coast. In his mind Luigi had struck gold and from that time on no one could convince him that the olive trees were wrong about anything. He would have jumped off the Tarpeian Rock if the trees had told him to do so. And the villagers thought *I* was crazy! For whatever reason I didn't fit in, and I didn't need to because I didn't really like anybody. I'd sit in my little house at my loom weaving linens by day and I couldn't help overhearing all the village gossip through my window, but it didn't concern me so I didn't carry it any further, and I certainly didn't give them any new fodder to cultivate about me. They always said the same old things anyway: *she's an odd one; no one wanted to marry her, she's a witch; she bakes for a secret lover!* Hah! That last one always got me laughing. Secret lover, indeed. He'd have to be suffering from advanced cataracts; remember, I was no irresistible beauty for all it mattered.

Life had presented no opportunity for a husband and children, though I loved children very much. That is why at night, after all the silly villagers had shuttered themselves into their fragrant little homes asleep near their livestock, I'd take out my flour and sugar, some cocoa powder and ground chili powder and I'd make some tasty little cookies. While the cookies were still warm I'd wrap them in some new cloths and take them along with a bundle of swaddling linens in a basket to the big house in the next village. It was called La Casa di Bambini Abbandonati; that was where a group of spinsters lived together and cared for abandoned infants, to save them from the Roman custom of *patria potestas*, that deplorable (but perfectly acceptable) practice of infanticide. People throwing away newborns (like Remus and Romulus), tossing them into the Tiber or outright killing them – honestly! Each little one deserved a chance to grow up, didn't they? The spinsters would leave the side door unlocked so I could come inside with my basket filled with cookies and linens for the babies. Sometimes the ladies and I would sit and chat and I told them that they were making the world a better place to live in because they made a home for the unwanted. They were probably the closest thing I had to friends that at the time. They would sometimes let me cradle an infant to sleep. Oh, there is nothing that brings more comfort to an old soul than to embrace a brand new one dropped straight down from heaven.

## 3

## *The Legend of Old Befana*

Oh yes, did I mention that I am a legend? In the old days all it took to become a legend was longevity of spirit, but folks nowadays are instant legends. Look at the covers of magazines at the supermarket, or the headlines of any "news" journals. Legends are so common that they can no longer be distinguished from celebrities or hoodlums. The primary difference is that my legend is old, just like me, tossed down from the past like a dusty heirloom, but I'm no celebrity. The modern "legends" consider themselves to be stars, like novae, bursting into stardom, shining their egotistical eminence into the future! It's funny, actually, what they take pride in! They are the sexiest people alive (whatever that means); they gain fame for pretending to be someone else better than anyone else; they're the most popular liar and win a prestigious post in government; they commit unspeakable crimes and people talk about them nonstop for days. They are legends and their names become a household word. Me? I'm just old.

Most people don't know about the legend of *Old Befana*, some do, but only if they are aware of what actually did happen. The legend grew out of a few facts – namely, an eccentric old lady who lived alone, baked cookies, grew hot peppers, wove some linens, and okay – was a little overzealous about cleaning the house, and because one night a unique star changed the entire course of life forever. I used to carry a broom around with me for many reasons. The arid climate in southern Italy can result in a lot of dust which is in desperate need of some rain to wash it away, but for those times when the clouds were stingy, a broom exercised night and day could keep the grit under control. There was another reason for carrying that old broom around: if ill-bred brutes began to taunt or threaten me, a broom handle dealt severely to the head of the perpetrator could work wonders at keeping them away. And those are just the tidbit, insignificant details about the old lady that lived in an obscure and unremarkable village during what turned out to be a very remarkable time in the history of the world. I played no part in the events which made the story remarkable – this is important to remember, mind you; I was just an ordinary, lonely old peasant woman minding my own business when something happened that changed just about everything, including my meaningless life. I was not some figure of notoriety, some member of a royal family or a woman of any considerable talents; I was just me, a life-worn, dried up old recluse living out my days, one at a time, waiting for the sands in the glass to run out. The last thing I ever expected was to become a world-traveler who actually had no choice but to *do something with my life!*

There was nothing new under the sun from one day to the next. The same wind that circled the earth and carried cold temperatures, snow, warmth, or rain did not produce anything new in my life. It was always the same raindrops or snowflakes that fell on my head time and time again. But, that night something happened that changed the way we looked at everything. At first it didn't seem like a night that was different than any other. It didn't appear to be spectacular in any way except that a terribly bitter cold snap had overtaken the village. The olive trees were glazed with ice and the air seemed to crackle as it gave in to an oppressive freeze. Upon rising that morning, I brought in some extra wood for the fire, cleaned my house, wove a few linens, ground up some strands of peppers into chili powder and made a large pot of pepper tea. Nothing outside moved that day; no one could be seen on the streets, not even the wild dogs that looked for scraps of food. The stillness was deafening. As night fell the village seemed to have gone into hibernation, without a sound to be heard, not even from the goats or sheep. The stoniness of the hardened world was eerie, even to someone like me. The village felt much like a burial ground and we were just dark, cold souls with no chance of anything springing into life, lying motionless, not knowing what to do. Outside my hut I saw that some icicles were hanging from the roof tiles so I wrapped myself in a heavy shawl and took my broom outside to knock down the spears of ice lest they impaled me when I went out in the morning. Once outside I took in a long, deep breath and for some reason it didn't feel as bad out there as I thought. It wasn't so unbearable that I couldn't walk over to the spinsters' house. I just needed to bundle up a little better than usual.

I finished up my chores, baked some cookies, filled the basket and grabbed my broom. Even on a night like this one couldn't be too careful – some thug might try to steal the cookies meant for the babies. Some of the little ones were getting older and teething now and my cookies made them feel better. Thankfully, the wind was blowing in the direction I was walking; it helped to have an unseen force pushing my steps a little faster. As I ascended the low hills that led to the next village, I saw a group of people walking on the road below me. Are they crazy, I thought? Don't they know it is cold out here tonight? Where on earth are they going? They were not the locals from any nearby village, I could see that. I'd never seen them before and some of them were dressed quite strangely in garments made of colorful fabrics I'd never seen before in my life. They must be the fancy people from the north, I thought. They even wore headgear that seemed to reflect the light of the moon. There was no moon that night but there was a star the likes of which I'd never seen before which caught my attention because it was so large and bright. These people were a strange sight but I didn't think they were marauders. They weren't hiding behind rocks waiting to pounce on me; they were too orderly and serene. They seemed to be following that star! I descended the hill and approached them carefully.

"You, there, where are you going?" I asked them. The entourage stopped when they heard me, but they said nothing. I repeated my question. "It's late and it's cold. Why are you out on a night like this?"

Finally, a young boy guiding one of the donkeys stopped for only a moment. He looked at me carefully, his eyes shining with some sort of insight that he wanted to both protect and share.

"Where are you all going?" I asked again.

He pursed his lips and then his eyes widened. "We are following the directions of the wise men that told us where to find the newborn baby."

"There are many newborn babies at that house down in that village over there. You're going the wrong way," I told him.

He shook his head. "He is not there. This baby is a newborn king."

"Oh," I replied. "Oh, then I'm sure he has many riches and servants if he is a king." The youth looked deeply into my eyes. "He is born in poverty in a stable with animals we've been told. He has no servants. He has nothing. We are taking him some gifts."

"Oh," I replied again. "Why are you going to see this newborn baby king? If he is so poor what can he possibly do for you, or for any of us?"

The youth turned from me and began to walk again but he kept talking. "He has come to show us the way to a new kingdom, one where all the poor, and only the poor, can enter.

He is a savior. You may come if you like." He continued walking to keep pace with the group.

"But I have nothing to bring him. He is a king and I have nothing to bring a king."

"He has already given you what you need to bring," said the youth. "You cannot bring him anything more."

I did not understand what this child meant. I didn't understand any of this. These people were foolish, it seemed. But they also seemed genuine; on a night like this they were not afraid to be following some unseen path as if their hearts could see what my eyes could not.

I stood, frozen in place, and watched them scale the hills ahead. Though it was icy cold and late into the night they seemed warmed and invigorated by something within, some deep understanding of their destination. I looked behind me at my old village. There was nothing there for me really. I wanted to see the kingdom that only the poor may enter. I wanted to see this newborn baby king. *I have some cookies and swaddling linens,* I thought. *Perhaps this night I can go to him instead. I do not know how to find him, but maybe the messengers will guide me. I want to go; now that I have heard about him I long to find him, no matter how long it takes me on this journey, if it takes the rest of my life.*

Old Befana, that's me, on my way to seek this newborn king and stopping along the way to offer my cookies or whatever I have to the poor infants and children that I come across along the way. That is how the legend of Old Befana began. The legend travels during the Christmas season, the time when the little king, the one called Emmanuel, Jesus the Christ, was born. The legend travels to bring gifts to all children just in case that child happens to be *the one.*

I don't think those villagers ever missed me. Maybe they thought I ran off with that secret lover in the middle of the night. There are many ways to keep a person alive once they've gone. Rumors are only one way, I suppose. If it's a person we love we keep them alive in our memories. We hear their voices, see their smiles, feel their touch, and their very presence. We remember what they've said when they were happy or angry or sad. They live on in the gift of love – that relationship – forever a mother, a father, a friend, a spouse. Sometimes they come to us in dreams; they inspire us or caution us. And many times, when we feel alone they continue to remind us that we are not and we never will be alone. They take away the fear of nothing.

Legends are kept alive in much the same way. People keep them alive through stories retold, time and again, through the traditions they prompt, and through people that carry on their mission. The tales, repeated at a time when they are most needed, bring comfort and consolation. Legends have a life of their own, once material in their earthly presence they continue as inspiration. It has happened with other legendary figures besides me. Legends like me carry a certain lore that makes us who we are in a fixed and perennial state but we'll talk about that some other time.

# 4

## Old Befana's New Adventure

I now seem to be permanently dressed in a dark green dress with some red accents here and there, a little too pretty for me, actually. Not my style. I don't remember ever owning this dress; my dress was always black because it was supposed to be slimming. Don't laugh; it's not vanity, really, because I was perfectly aware of my true appearance – a little fluffy around the edges at that time. Someone that enjoyed baking cookies as much as I did tends to eat a few more cookies than she should. However, I have become quite accustomed to this green and red dress, the colors of Christmas! It brings to mind the night that changed my life. Green has something to say about life like those trees that don't die in the winter and red is for love, something I never felt from anyone nor really felt I had ever shared with another soul, not until that night. The life I lived before that first Christmas seems to be fading from my memory; all I know is that I was by myself with my own routines and life was quiet, and since that night I never know what to expect and I never get a moment's peace. My life is full of people, adventures, encounters, and yes, even drama! That night I encountered some*thing*, some*one* new, new to me anyway and everything changed, even my dress and it's a reminder of who I am now. This new desire to *love* is my gift.

Between that night of shining stars and no moon and this day filled with bright sunlight, a world of people suddenly lit up and stirred. One birth, out of so many, propelled humanity into new and deeper understandings. One child was born to fine-tune the routines of life, to teach us how to truly live, and to have the life we were meant to have. He let us peek inside the human heart and see what it was made of, and weren't we surprised! That glimpse has had us struggling ever since. Oh, the things we've been trying to *understand*. I may have always been a simpleton, but believe me, what I've been learning along the way is exactly what I was supposed to learn. With each encounter there is a deeper glimpse.

The circumstance leading me to this new place began with a woman named Margaret, a strikingly beautiful woman with dark hair and eyes the color of my Italian coffee and skin that looks like the petal of a rose. She is remarkable, but heaven help me, she is very unhappy. The difficulty she is enduring is quite different from that which I once experienced. I had always lived in solitude, perhaps by fate but most likely by choice, yet Margaret suffers from loss which is a deep bruise beneath the skin of loneliness. I didn't know her when she was happy but I can see and hear her memories.

In the sitting room of the stately manor where she lives a ray of light streams through the panel windows and exposes a photograph that sits on the mahogany mantelpiece. In the photo, wisps of Margaret's hair drift in front of her eyes as she looks up at a handsome young man named David. She is dressed in a vintage style Edwardian gown and he in a dinner suit from the same era. They are standing in front of a Sweet Bay Magnolia in full bloom. The only thing that surpasses the showy white flowers in this photo is the burst of promise in the eyes of the newly wedded couple. They look to be madly in love, as hopefully everyone does on their wedding day. At the time they were wed, Margaret managed her family's business affairs in Barrington Industries and this is where she'd met David Livingston, one of the executives. An hour after his first glimpse of Margaret, David had turned to his friend, George, and said, "I'm gonna marry that girl."

On the fifteenth of June the society pages of *The London Times* announced the news of the glamorous wedding: Barrington Heiress Weds the Last of the Cornwall Livingstons. In the picture David looks like the world is at his feet. Margaret, however, has the quiet look of tenderness, the kind that awaits the kiss of life.

# 5

## *Margaret*

Tonight I have mustered up the courage to venture out to the theater alone. It has been quite some time since I last attended a show. I remember the last play I attended was with David and we saw *Caesar and Cleopatra* at the Metropolitan. He thought I would enjoy it, after all it was supposedly a love story, but I felt it had illustrated the political side of that relationship, and the fact that each ruler had his and her own agenda. It didn't seem like love to me; the agenda always came first and the relationship served a prioritized set of purposes. David and I had spent half the night discussing the play after we returned home. His main point was that men have many layers when it comes to love and that they can perform equally well on all tiers. Women, however, generally have fewer levels and are often "out of their depth" in political and intimate relationships with men. I maintained, at the time, that the level where men and women come together to love one another should never be complicated by other agendas; love should be kept separate. In the end I think he'd patronized me and said that my romantic side was what he loved the most about me, but acknowledged that purity of love should never be tarnished by self-interest. Were Caesar and Cleopatra ever in "love?" We'd both agreed they were not. It was unlikely that either had loved any person more than they loved power.

After several dress changes I decided on a blue velvet gown trimmed with white Venetian lace that I wore to Mary's wedding six years ago. I still have the matching beaded reticule which is actually my favorite part of the ensemble. I do not care about the latest fashion trends and I do not care how many people this evening might be staring for one reason or another. I see that I am the fifth in line at the box office. A young woman in front of me whispers something into her gentleman's ear and then lets out a small titter while covering her mouth with her handkerchief. The gentleman leaves a delicate kiss on the young woman's forehead. Charming. I am trying to see past them to the box office. Has it opened yet? Will this line ever begin to move? There is another couple at the front of the line, an older couple not nuzzling close together just simply holding hands waiting for the box office window shade to rise. The woman says something to the man that makes him throw his head back and laugh in that perennial sort of way that older couples share, a quip that has made him laugh repeatedly for many years. I stare forward not daring to look behind me; I certainly do not wish to draw attention to myself as people may think I am awaiting someone and when no one arrives it will be quite evident that I have come to the theater alone. It is best if I simply try to blend obscurely into a crowd of couples intent upon each other's presence.

Thank God the box office window has opened and the line is beginning to move. Once inside where the lights are dim I am desperately eager to relax and fade into the velvet the chairs and sip a small glass of sherry before the play begins. When the ticket master hands me the evening's billet for *The Duchess of Padua*, I scurry through the lobby of the Sophronia Theater where a large Rochester brass chandelier hangs prominently from the ceiling. I am attempting to stay to the left of the lights to remain less visible and maneuver my way through the Corinthian columns that support the inner porticos. The sense of security that these beautiful structures provide both for their sturdiness and their ability to obscure provides some comfort, but my heart is racing. It is always this way when I leave the house these days though there is no immediate threat to my safety. It has merely become my habit to suspect the unknown around every corner. There was a time when the knowledge that tragedies only happened to other people provided me with a confidence that I had nothing to fear from life. I'd ignored the reality that those "other" people might have felt the same way at some point before their misfortune. Life can change without invitation.

The ancient lovers that adorn the bass reliefs along the atrium walls have dubious emotions etched into their frozen faces which beckon some degree of empathy. What were their stories, their fears, their apprehensions? Though their names have been lost to time, the inheritance of passion is a natural part of being human and lingers in their expressions. Even the amiable white statues at the edges of the vestibule appear to be coddling a secret sentiment that I once understood, but time and people and life itself can alter the colors of one's life unlike these figures whose static moment of wonder is impressed into marble forever.

Suddenly, I hear my name called out. I'd feared this possibility.

"Margaret!" Oh dear, it is Beth Farnsworth and her husband Henry, Minister of State for Education. They are directly in my path and I cannot avoid them.

"Margaret, darling, it is so good to see you out and about." She air-kisses both of my cheeks but her eyes are seeking David, to see if he has accompanied me or if I am still alone. Henry extends his hand to greet me politely and is quick to verbalize the obvious.

"Is David not here this evening?" Beth visibly elbows him and he clears his throat. "Right," he says. "I concur with Beth, my dear; it is good to see you this evening." I make my pleasantries as quickly as possible and excuse myself by declaring that I must find my seat.

By the time I reach the heavy red curtains at the entrance to my box seat my nerves are a bit rattled. I do not believe I shall attempt to do this again. What I wish is for my presence to be invisible and irrelevant not an opportunity for wagging tongues.

Though the theater fills quickly it is not filled to capacity this evening. At last I can exhale when the lights are dimmed as if my suspended breathing had fueled the lamps. The play begins. I suppose I came this evening because I was intrigued by the idea that observing the tragedies of others is far more preferable than enduring one's own.

*"Will you not speak to me?*
*Love me a little: in my girlish life*
*I have been starved for love, and kindliness*
*Has passed me by."*

When all is lost and nothing may be recovered, it is then that the human heart is free to harden without bearing the burden of its flowing duties. Guido and Beatrice understood this *raison d'être* to the extent that many lovers have also come to understand it. By the time the characters meet with their ineffaceable destinies, the observers may yawn, fan themselves, or resort to an earlier conversation that may have been interrupted by a moment's curiosity. For them the play completely lacked fire and obsession, but for me the foolishness of Tennyson is evidently understated: it is *not* better to have loved and lost than never to have loved at all. I can hear my internal conviction repeat itself – *it would have been better if I had never known such love.* Pangs of regret immediately thud against my senses. Living with the loss of this intense love is an unmerciful death prolonged each day by memory. I snatch my reticule and leave the theater without further delay.

# 6

## *Old Befana*

In all my existence I have never seen such desolation – not in a *person*. Margaret is like a wasteland, not the kind that had always been uninhabited; hers is more of an aftershock. One can see the remnants of past joy, music, laughter, love, surprises and even lightheaded whimsy in her dark eyes, but now these relics of life lie beneath the fragments of ruined happiness. Poor thing. Some people can heal, others just die; you can see the heaviness she carries and what's bothersome is what you don't see.

Back in my day, I knew a woman named Irena, or was it Ileana? Maybe it was Giorgina – pah, I can't remember anymore. She was much older than me at the time. What I remember vividly is that she sold figs on market days in my old hometown. At the time I thought "What's the matter with this lady? She is cold and fake" – no, no, not like a statue, because statues represent someone once warm and real. No, Irena, or whatever her name was, seemed more like the limestone before it is fashioned into something people can appreciate or relate to. I'd judged that if she had a heart at all underneath those hard bones, it was the size of a fig seed, and not of much use. But the woman sold good figs. Actually, she grew the very best figs for miles around and that was the only reason people came to her on market days. Her demeanor was always calm and steady; she never got riled up like some of us did from that part of Italy; she just had a scary peacefulness about her like she knew something the rest of us didn't know. That was why, as good as they tasted, I never bought her figs. I didn't trust her. She never looked mad or unhappy, or anything like that; it was her smile that stiffened the hairs on my moles. She had the smile of a lizard, not a friendly smile at all; it literally sliced her face from ear to ear. *Spaventoso*. It was enough to make you jump if you saw her.

Like me, Irena never married, never had any children and did not seem to have any family lying about. She was alone and solitude can do something to a person's face after a while. When people read the pallor of solitude on someone's face it is a look they don't want to understand, it is something they fear. It is easier to turn away than to infect it with companionship. Many years later, I learned of Irena's life. She'd grown up in La Casa di Bambini Abbandonati when there were only two or three spinsters caring for the little castoffs and there was very little food to eat because, at that time, there were so many babies abandoned to the backwoods, left to cry, starve, freeze, or be eaten by wild animals. Some were smothered first and that was meant to be better, but later I'll tell you why they weren't better off in the long run. Irena never talked to people; she just smiled that fiendish smile of hers and sold her figs until the day she fell asleep under one of her fig trees and never woke up. I also learned much later that she would take bushels of figs to the unwanted children. The spinsters would eat them; they said that figs gave the babies loose bowels. Well, I'd misjudged old Irena and that was a result of my own blinkered thinking. I felt so bad that I hadn't offered her a kind word that I now try to make mental lists of kind words I could say to people so that at least I have a kind vocabulary to work with.

This woman, Margaret, however, did not grow up in the same circumstances as Irena. Margaret had a family, quite an affluent one with all the amenities and privileges of a comfortable life. But Margaret's secure life had not been without its problems. The thing is problems can be solved, tragedies cannot. Everyone silently knows that tragedies are problems that are punctuated by a dreadful finality. Realizing a good result from a sad set of circumstances takes a lot of love, not the kind that sounds good but the kind that hurts. It didn't make sense to me at first either. I never had the chance to learn about it in a family.

Margaret has a twin sister named Mary. "Two sides of the same dirty coin" their mother would smile and say. The twins had never gotten along. Mary had always resented the twenty minutes between them. It was all a matter of *positioning*, Mary had reasoned, not a question of true merit that the advantages of being first-born should be applied to the way in which Margaret (in-utero) had shrewdly lodged herself closer to the birth opening. From the time they could speak they bickered and squabbled over everything imaginable: clothing, for instance, even if identical in color, fabric and embellishments, Mary would be furious at having to dress in the same substandard dress as her sister who was *beneath her* right from the womb. The situation didn't get any better with the birth of Anne, the youngest child, for then Mary was caught in the middle of two commanding forces: the oldest who would inherit the lion's share, and the youngest who grabbed up all the parental affection with her coquettish charms.

The three Barrington sisters had been named after some of Scotland's most interesting queens. Their mother hailed from the Midlothian region of that country and it seemed that her loyalties remained with her kinfolk. Margaret was named for Saint Margaret of Scotland, who, even though she'd been an English princess at birth, went on to become a the kind of queen who helped transform a brute of a husband and tamed the Scottish people who were always ready to do battle. Mary's namesake was the ill-fated queen whose greatest misfortune had been the timing of her own birth following that of her cousin, Elizabeth I of England, and the threat which her very existence represented to the tyrant daughter of Henry VIII. The youngest Barrington was named for the last monarch of Scotland, Anne Stuart.

It sounds to me like Mary suffers from a histrionic personality of the most unattractive kind, demanding the center of all attention, trying to make herself out to be irresistible to men, even though she'd married quite an honorable man of a good (and patient) nature, and provoking people into quarrels which would ultimately make her look like the helpless victim of circumstance at which point her honorable husband would come to her rescue.

Anne was sweet, quite amiable, but not thought to be the brightest jewel in the crown. She had a knack for steering clear of her sisters and avoiding the fray whenever possible by playing alone with a train set and building blocks. When Anne came of age she'd married a wealthy merchant whose business was firmly established in India and off she went, away from the endless drama caused by her sisters.

These days, Margaret finds it easier to avoid Mary altogether. For many years she had actually tried to forge some kind of a truce with her twin and establish a rapport that might encourage a sisterly bond, but Mary had become too adept at provoking Margaret into a fresh version of some old argument. "You are so manipulative" Mary had said the last time they'd spoken. "I am manipulative? I try various ways to have a relationship with my sister, and this makes me manipulative?" Margaret had shaken her head. "I have searched for activities that we might both enjoy, topics of conversation that we might engage in peacefully, but heaven forbid such diabolical acts of manipulation because the truth of the matter is that you want us to remain at odds with one another. I have done my very best, Mary." Mary had laughed in her face. "Hah," she'd said, "I can think of plenty of sisters who could have been better than you." Margaret had faced her twin, "Name just one person who had *you* for a sister that might have handled it much better," she'd said, and she turned and walked away. She regretted her words deeply and wished she could find a way to make amends with Mary. Margaret loved her sister, but Mary knew how to cause fresh pain to old scars.

I came to Margaret through something called a "jumble sale." It had been a temperate spring day and Margaret had decided to get out of the house for the first time since her world had changed. These days she rarely leaves the house and never accepts callers. People stopped visiting after a while, but on that particular day, Margaret had decided she needed some fresh air; I think her emptiness was becoming itchy. Usually, she mapped out her routines in order to move smoothly from one day into the next for she could no longer imagine an existence other than one governed by predictability. She never seems to give herself over to a life of expectations or hopes. She has fought hard each day to keep from dreaming about a different way to live. Dreams are that spark that light up hope, and poor Margaret no longer has either dreams or hopes.

For some reason that's where I came in. Statuettes and figurines rarely represent a figment of pure imagination; they always seem to carry the character of someone who was once real. My image comes with a satchel filled with sweet ideas about moving forward and a few seeds of inspiration to plant when I see the chance. What is most important about this job is to find a way to do the caring thing. I understand this now because I've learned that everything will eventually be all right. One day, when you least expect it, a star in the sky can change your life. I didn't know that before but you're never too old to learn. Once your fears wear you down and life's crusty edges begin to dampen, your heart becomes a little more supple to work with!

# 7

## *Margaret*

When Ivy walked into the study this morning, she did not have a feather-duster in hand as usual; rather, she'd carried in a countenance of unease which seemed to deposit a layer of unrest upon every object within. Normally, Ivy goes about her household duties without complaint or disturbance, but on this occasion she seemed disoriented, quite unlike herself. I have a deep fondness for Ivy; she is one of those guileless creatures who have an understanding of contentment in any circumstance, quite the opposite of those who are unhappy regardless of the blessings they receive. She has been the steady wave that has swept comfort into my life and eased away the fragments of wreckage.

Ivy had come into service as a young girl of fourteen and was given delicate duties and simple tasks for some time. She has always worked diligently and cheerfully at any new task no matter the difficulty. As other servants took their leave because of personal discontent, or were dismissed because their services were no longer required, Ivy remained like a fixture that had always been a part of this house on Chestnut Hill. Where once my home was brimming with family, friends, and gallant acquaintances, it is now down to the two of us and it suits me just fine, but I sensed on this particular morning that Ivy's outlook had changed somehow. She lingered at each of the oak bookcases for some time fussing with the tidiness of the books.

"Ivy? Is there something you wish to ask me?" I coached carefully as she stared at the shelves with a faraway look.

"Ma'am" she replied softly. She bit her bottom lip struggling, it seemed, to find just the right approach. I didn't press her. I'd known Ivy for fifteen years and I trusted her ability to speak without coercion. Finally, she began:

"It is my sister, Ma'am; I know I've never spoken of her. I have a sister; her name is Colleen. She is younger than me by five years. She moved here to London a couple of years ago but now, I'm afraid, she's taken ill." The very words taken ill, I realized, were the ones she was struggling with.

"I am very sorry, Ivy. Is there something she needs?"

"She can no longer work or care for her little one, Ma'am. She is taken to her bed. I think she could use my help, Ma'am. I'm sorry to ask. If I could be spared for a few hours each day to help my sister, to help with the little one? Her husband, he's gone, Ma'am." Ivy had kept her eyes on her hands the entire time she'd spoken and wisps of her dark hair were in collusion with her need to avert her gaze. She knew I would grant her any amount of time she needed; she was not afraid to ask this personal favor. Her fears stemmed from her loyalty, her need to be here for me and I could see that she felt quite torn. I knew this about her, when everyone else had deserted this home in one way or another it was Ivy who had remained. She stood in silence waiting for me to speak. She had never asked me for any personal favors and now she simply wanted some time to tend to her own family matters. I was not even aware that she had a sister. She had been devoting herself to me exclusively for so long now and I was completely unaware of her personal life. I sighed.

"Give me a moment," I said.

"Yes, Ma'am," and she quietly left the study.

I sat at my father's old bureau desk and tapped my fingers on its sturdy oak surface. This desk had such family history. It had once belonged to my grandfather who had built up the tea and tobacco company from the remnants of his grandfather's textile industry. Such a variety of work had settled into the soul of this old desk. My grandfather had kept only a small line of textile while developing the tobacco imports which seemed to be more lucrative. He was a quirky old man, I remember. He had a fondness for statues; his study reflected his taste in various works of art he accumulated on his travels. The porcelain Columbine and Pierrot figurines adorned the baroque table near the window and the light always seemed to illuminate their coy smiles. The pair had always reminded me of young lovers planning an elusive tryst. Each member of the family had added their own taste in various ways so that eventually the tables, shelves, and corners were teeming with cultural diversity.

My addition to this priceless collection was a ragamuffin antique, an elderly lady who seemed awkward in her current surroundings. She sat on the shelf staring at me with her mischievous smirk. Since the day I'd been left to my own devices, I'd craved solitude like a drug. I was completely dependent on the freedom that comes from emptiness. I'd discovered this figurine at St. Bart's jumble sale several months after my solitary addiction began. Somehow the presence of this quirky vagrant comforted me in a solidarity sort of way. I picked up the figurine and stared into her painted eyes. She was a charmingly hideous-looking thing, not like all the seductive pre-Raphaelite statues that could be found throughout this home since my childhood. This statuette was hunched over, ragged, and clothed in tattered fabric from the distant past. She was an unkempt old hag, but there was something so charismatic about her that I just knew I had to have her the minute I'd seen her. When one requires complete isolation a statue as a friend poses no threat.

My little statue had an itinerant look about her, a look of possibilities sparkling in her eyes. "You're on some kind of mission, aren't you?" I asked my little friend. "You are not portrayed as someone who is frozen in the state of ecstasy like so many of your cohorts. You are on your way somewhere, with a knapsack on your back and a broom in your hand, and that little grin that guards some sort of secret you're withholding that perhaps you are meant to deliver. Hmmm… Fine. I don't need to understand you in order to like you. I never have. You always help me clear my cluttered mind."

"Ivy?" I knew she would be lingering nearby for an answer. I set my figurine back down on the shelf with its back to me facing the window just as Ivy reentered the study.

"Yes, Ma'am," she said expectantly.

"Please, sit. I've decided to give you leave for two hours in the morning and two hours in the afternoon to help your sister." I stopped speaking. I did not wish to say what my conscience was nagging at me to suggest. I tried with difficulty to suppress it. I have cared about this young girl from the day she came to us.

"Oh, thank you, Ma'am. I am so grateful…" I held up my hand so that Ivy would not continue. I wanted to hurry and dismiss her from the room before I said something I knew I would regret. She took my signal and stood up to leave. She is grateful for so very little.

"Ivy." I bit my lip.

"Yes, Ma'am?"

"This house is enormous, and little used. Would it be more helpful to bring your sister and her little one here to stay until her health improves? The servants' quarters are terribly vacant." Ivy did not speak. She did not even seem to breathe. I think I was regretting it already. But this was Ivy, the one who'd mercifully remained for my sake, who now needed a favor. She seemed to be losing color in her face.

"But, Ma'am. My sister is sick. I wouldn't want her or the little one to disturb you."

I didn't reply. I stood and faced the window toward the same view as the little statue of my old hag. I looked outside blankly without seeing Chestnut Hill, or passersby, or the old mill across the road. I was staring into my past, though it was always so painful remembering all those who were sick at one time or another in this home. All that loss. But now I was losing the fight to retain the stone garden that my heart had become and I believed this little hag was responsible.

# 8

## *Old Befana*

At least three things are clear at the beginning of every journey; the rest is a revelation waiting to unfold like a pleated hand fan that opens into a painted scene. First, you can only begin with what dwells within you; other things can be obtained or lost along the way but everyone takes that first step inwardly. Second, journeys require change regardless of your destination: it may be a change in your perspective, your goals, your determination, or the way you deal with setbacks; – a journey of any kind involves *movement*; sitting in the same spot doesn't make for a journey. Third, there is a solitary aspect to a journey; no one can make the exact same journey as your own even if they're tagging along, but you are never completely alone because journeys of any kind depend on influences from some outside force, seen or unseen. No one journeys through a vacuum. Ancient folks like me have always understood these three things. A way to connect to the space in which you move is essential to a journey, whether it's a connection to nature, time, variations, or people - something influences your ability to keep going or to turn back.

Personally, I'd never given any thought to venturing outside of the little circle that I called home. My little life was enough for me. The things that lived within me? I had some fears. I didn't know how to relate to others very well, so I kept to myself a lot. I made up for fear by hanging on to other things that brought me comfort, such as the familiar aroma of my hometown, the sweet biscuits I'd bake, the occasional visits to the spinsters and babies, the livestock traipsing down the lane, the olives, fruits, and fish on market days. These pieces of my life I carried from one day into the next like ingrained habits. They're all I had with me when I took my first steps. What changed along the way were my notions about things, having the eyes to see my life as either a blessing or an act of endurance. I have to admit I didn't think there was much purpose to the whole business of living; it was just something to get through from one day to the next. And finally, the lonely idea I had to shake off was that no one gave a ripe fig one way or the other what happened to me. None of this makes any sense until you see the bigger view, which you cannot see if you stay in a little circle. Until I took the first step I was stuck, one day feeling content, and the next day wondering why I couldn't understand the point of it all, much like a small caged animal. That's no way to live. When that star grabbed my attention everything changed. I wish everyone could see that when you take in the view from where the stars are shining, nothing ever looks the same again.

# 9

## *Ivy*

I would never have imagined that my mistress would open this door of opportunity. She has always been kind to me; even during the bad times when she was so overwhelmed she had never spoken an unkind word to me. She'd remained formal and commanded the authority she possessed yet she'd never expressed any callousness, at least not in my direction. I thought she might find any number of reasons why all problems should be kept at bay but I never expected that she would invite my troubles into her home. That was how I knew. I'd always suspected that underneath her rigid and severe character she was a sensitive soul. It was the only reason I had been able to muster up the courage to ask if I could help my sister Colleen. I was frightened to ask, not because I suspected that my mistress would say no out of cruelty, but because I feared that it would hurt her to say *yes*. I simply didn't know what else to do. Colleen has been unwell since she and her little one came over here from Ireland. Danny, her husband, had brought them here because he'd found work but then he left them without a word. Colleen had been trying to cope these past few months at the workhouse for women and caring for the child but this past week she collapsed. I'd been taking her my share of food from dinner to help her a bit when the mistress goes out but I could see last night that she can no longer get out of bed. Little Nollaig, whom she calls Nolly, always sits on the floor beside her mother whispering to the doll I'd made her from some old rags. Sometimes she cries for her mother to play but more often she whimpers out of hunger. It breaks my heart. My mistress's kindness has taken my breath away. To bring them here – *here* to this house, it seems unreal. The servants' wing hasn't been used these last two years and it lies on the opposite side from the family quarters. If Nolly should cry I cannot let her disturb my Mrs. Livingtson. I pray, Lord, that the sound of a crying child never reaches my mistress's ears. She is so gracious to offer this support. She wants nothing more than peace at any cost.

But how am I to move Colleen and Nolly to this house. I can carry the child but I do not think that Colleen can walk all this way. I cannot bring myself to ask my mistress for any more favors. I see through the window of the study that she has gone out this evening and from what she said she will be gone for some time. She often takes long walks after dark along the fringes of Chestnut Hill where the winding path leads down to the Briarwood Commons where scattered residents take their evening constitution. She asks for no supper when she plans one of her strolls; once in a while she craves the fellowship of darkness without the weight of complete solitude. I tidy up the study quickly. The statuette of the old woman holding a broom has been moved once again, this time facing the window. I cannot understand my mistress' fondness for this little talisman of poverty. Sometimes she sits on the desk; at other times she is lodged between books on the shelf; once in a while I find her on the mantle in front of the mirror but most often she is sitting on the sill looking out, almost as if she is pondering her next move. The broom she carries is like the oar of a mariner, whose purpose it is to steer her way forward. She seems intent on looking toward hope. The broom, ah yes, perhaps a couple of brooms will be useful to me as well!

A bed sheet from the upstairs cupboard tied securely between two brooms may serve as some sort of gurney for transport. Poor Colleen, she deserves better. And little Nolly? Perhaps she can walk a ways. I do not know how to make this work, but I shall try, and I must do it soon while the sky remains clear.

***

Colleen is shivering when I arrive at the shelter. The matron of the workhouse, Mrs. Preen, is trying to indicate that Colleen's presence has become a burden and the child is too young to work and compensate for the rations they receive. I explain that I have come to take them both away. The matron raises an eyebrow and seems reluctant to understand. "I am her sister, Ivy," I explain. "I am her next of kin. I have come to remove her from these quarters and the child, too." But the matron looks me up and down and mentions the five shillings that would settle things for whatever food Colleen received while living in this dank and airless house for women these past two weeks since Colleen became seriously ill. She eyes the old wheelbarrow that I found in the old gardener's shed. I'd cleaned off all the dirt and cobwebs and scrubbed it down with soap and water, taking care because its age and frailty needed a delicate hand if it were to hold the small gurney and the weight of my ailing sister. The matron takes my five shillings and turns away. I help Colleen onto the makeshift cot as gently as I can.

Then Nolly begins to cry softly and I hug her closely and kiss her forehead. She is just a wisp of a thing; she has Colleen's deep violet eyes that look like pools of wine on a moonlit night; there seems to be very little whites around her penetrating eyes. Her hair is Danny's however, fine strands of golden, featherlike silk that curls and wafts without the aid of a breeze. Her dainty frame makes her seem more like a little doll than a child of four. She is shivering, too, like her mother. It isn't cold, it is fear. "Would you like to go with me to a pretty house, Nolly?" I ask her. She turns her head without replying and casts a worried look at her mother. "Mama can come, too, my sweet. Both of you are coming with me to a pretty house. Would you like that?" I ask again. This time she nods her head and grabs her mother's fingers. "Let's all go together. Are you okay to walk, my sweet?" She doesn't reply but makes for the door. She wants to leave this place without delay.

It is well past sunset by the time we reach Mulberry Street near the corner of Chestnut Hill. Nolly sniffles, especially when she drops a bag she is carrying, but she hasn't complained and she hasn't cried out. We are quite the spectacle, a woman being carted in a sheet tied between two brooms nestled into the hollow of an old wheelbarrow, with a small child desperately clutching the woman's fingers and a perspiring servant who keeps shifting her weight from side to side to carry their few belongings while steering clear of the nicer carriages that dominate the street. I wish to spare my mistress of the wagging tongues that will surely report such an abysmal sight to anyone that thrives on gossip in this community. She'd suffered quite enough of that in recent years and I certainly do not wish to add to the spiteful fodder. I turn quickly before we reach the house so that I can navigate my little migrant family through the woods and avoid as many meddlesome oglers as possible.

Once we are safely inside the back door near the kitchen, even Nolly seems confident that it is now safe to cry out. She lets out her pent-up steam while I help my sister into the chair near the stove. Oxtail soup is simmering in the pot and there is warm bread on the hob. "Is anyone hungry besides me?" I ask heartily. Nolly stops crying and looks up. Colleen opens her eyes and smiles. We sit silently in the corner of the kitchen and eat until we are satisfied, but suddenly Nolly seems frightened when she notices all the crumbs from the bread that have fallen to the floor. She spies the brooms near the door and quickly retrieves one of them from the bed sheet. It is twice her size but she has been taught how to use it. I am stunned but I let her sweep up her crumbs. She looks at me for approval with eyes steeped in fear. "Come here, my darling. Thank you for sweeping so beautifully. Would you like a sweet bun for your troubles?" Shooting a glance at her mother she is suspicious of my offer. Colleen has fallen asleep in her chair. I take one of the sweet buns from the cupboard and cut it in half. "You and I have done a lot of work this evening. We will share a sweet bun. When Mama wakes up we'll give her one, too." Nolly seems pleased and takes the sugary bread from my hand. As I help them to the room I have prepared for them both Nolly has collapsed from fatigue and trauma. My heart is full. They are here with me and they are safe.

# 10

## *Old Befana*

It was a time when everyone was trying to summon the inner artist, to capture the secrets of beauty by painting and sculpting the human form, by composing music that reminded the soul of our distant home, and by discovering new ways of solving problems and trying to get a better look at the stars. It was also a time when conflicts had more to do with salvaging sacred places and their treasures because this love of beauty consumed them. It was a time when thoughts and ideas were sparking in a thousand different directions at the same time; it was a time of human vitality – whether at its best or not, it was a momentum of rebirth. For the life of me, I can't be sure of the date because time no longer has structure in my head, but I know I was there, and I had a hard time keeping up with everything around me because everything seemed to be spinning in a whirlwind of imagination.

I guess I'm remembering it now because that was the time when someone had imagined my present unusual form. By the standards of those days he was an amateur, one of those sculptors, a rare sort without the usual hubris. But bless his twitchy heart he made me look better than I ever had before. I can forgive the fact that he was a northern Italian because he was not haughty, all-knowing, and pretentious like the rest; he'd sculpted an old, wrinkly hobo like me for instance. He wasn't too concerned with notoriety like some of those other fellas (like the one named for Michael the archangel!) who aspired to loftier creations. This guy – Pietro – he had a real job during the day; sculpting was more of a hobby. He worked for the court of those Medici dukes, one duke after another, day after day keeping records of their sales and purchases. But when Pietro came home, he kissed his wife, ate his *ceci al forno*, and then by the light of his candle he went to his back room for the evening and made things from clay, limestone, or even olive wood. He would work well into the night making small statues to give some sort of form to the people in the stories he had heard. Pietro needed to give shape to life. His favorite story was of that special night, the one where all the earth was changed because the caring God cared enough to become one of us. God no longer wanted to talk *through* people anymore he wanted to talk directly *to* us. Rather than hugging us with sunshine alone, he wanted to put his real arms around us and comfort us, heal us, and make us feel his love. He came down as a poor baby and he learned our language so he could use words to tell us how much he loved us and showed us in ways we could understand. Pietro believed that story that he had heard from the priests even though he hadn't been alive when it actually happened. So Pietro spent his nights in his dimly lit workshop enjoying a mental respite while God used his hands to make small figures. Pietro smiled when he saw a little donkey come out of the wood, the one that carried the exquisite carving of the Virgin Mary on the way to Bethlehem. He laughed when he saw the shepherd boy etched in marble because he had a surprised look on his face at seeing a spectacle in the sky that night. Pietro wept at the figure of Joseph whose face was humbled in the knowledge that God had asked *him* for a favor. Pietro spent countless hours carving, fashioning, chiseling, and molding the figures of kings, angels, innkeepers, animals, and children. He'd moved on to stories that themselves had taken shape around that miraculous night, like the story of that old bishop of Myra who had also lived during a pretty crazy time period. I remembered hearing that many people died during the reign of that loony Roman emperor because they wanted to believe the good news that the Christ child had preached about God's kingdom. Those Romans, they're rather territorial, you know, like that fellow Diocletian who razed churches to the ground, harassed, tortured, and killed people. He even passed laws to make it illegal for people to show their faith in ways that the caring God had asked them to. He wasn't the first, and he certainly would not be the last. Well, that bishop of Myra was a good man. He came into a world turned upside down and through his generosity and loving spirit he turned it right-side-up again. Legends abounded around Nicholas, too, for his charity, his compassion, his selflessness and his great love for the caring God's Son. He was a man who deserved to be given form out of the wood of an olive tree and remembered for his benevolence. I don't know what Pietro was thinking when he included me in his ministry and gave me shape and form. I'm just a very old lady in a constant state of searching.

Pietro had three sons. The oldest, Baldassare, had joined the Crusade of Nicopolis, a rather noble attempt to stop the people who did not believe in Christ Jesus from pushing their empire into new places and annihilating the people who did. Baldassare was one of three thousand men captured during this crusade and he'd never returned home. His father knew that defending a belief in Christ often meant the same kind of great sacrifice that he himself had made. He believed that a caring God was a God worth defending. His second son, Gaspare, had fallen in love with Gisella, a beauty from the campagna of Siena. He went to work for her father, to manage his vineyards and to earn her hand in marriage. Several years later he had died of St. Anthony's fire just one year after he married Gisella. Pietro's youngest, Melchiorre, had taken his vows and joined an order of Dominicans of the missionary variety, journeyed to the new world, and had not been heard from since.

Through his losses Pietro's heart became more devoted to the Baby Jesus. He had carved many, many figurines from his favorite story of the child's birth, but he had yet to carve the figure of the Christ child himself. Pietro looked into the faces of his neighbors' children and the infants of his kin but none alone could serve as a model for the Baby Jesus. To imagine the face of God would be his ultimate struggle; the desire burned fervently in his heart growing stronger each day, but how could the face of the creator burst into the face of a vulnerable child? The old man's imagination had roamed through many human features but found its roadblock in fashioning the face of the infant king. Pietro looked at me, with my wrinkly features and time-worn sagginess. *Are you looking at me for inspiration?* He picked me up and held me for a while. "Look at you," he said, "you are a traveler, a giver, maybe even some kind of messenger. Why do people do what they do? Why do you go around doing what you do?" He sighed heavily and set me down on the shelf with hundreds of figurines. I tried to give him the best answer I could: if someone's heart is acting freely they do what they do because they care. I don't know if he heard me.

He went back to sculpting and for the next few weeks he was working on a startling figure. He was using wood for this one; two pieces carved perpendicular to one another and then at the midpoint there was a figure that frightened me. It was the shape of a wounded man and Pietro spent many, many hours trying to carve his features just right. Night after night he bent over the dim light of his candle and scored the wood gently with his tools. With careful precision he etched the sinews of muscle in perfect detail. The face of the figure was carved to convey emotion not just human features. The arms and legs were given a gentle appearance and the entire figure seemed to possess an expression of surrender to an unknown desire. None of the rest of us seemed to garner this much concentrated attention; it seemed as if he was trying to give some sort of shape to *love*. Pietro handled this figure so delicately that it appeared to cause him pain as he shaped the arms that stretched out to the side and the legs that were forced tightly together. It was when I saw the tiny pegs driven into the hands to hold them to the horizontal piece of wood and the other peg pushed deeply through the feet to hold them to the vertical beam that I felt something open up in the core of my being, a longing to love this figure as much as Pietro seemed to love him. When at last a bristly crown had been placed on the figure's head, Pietro whispered something softly into the face of the figure and smiled. He wasn't talking *to* the statue; he was speaking beyond it. He and this sympathetic figure had become part of one another. Gently he arranged the figure between the statues of the Virgin Mary and Joseph. The wise men stood by with little gifts in their hands, the shepherds held their lambs close by, and Pietro nodded his head contentedly before he laid it down one last time to rest on his bench.

# 11

## *Margaret*

"Have your sister and her child settled in all right?" I'd asked Ivy one morning. "Fine, Ma'am, we are so grateful for your hospitality. I hope we haven't disturbed you at all."

"No, Ivy, there has been no disturbance. I'd wondered if your plans for them had changed." One would not know that the occupants of this house had doubled in the past few weeks. Ivy has been very diligent with her duties as usual, perhaps even more so, and has made certain that nothing has changed in our established routines. She is quite attentive and careful not to even mention her sister, and especially not the child. I don't even know if it is a boy or a girl, how old it is, or if it is well or sickly. All I know for certain is that the house remains as quiet as before. I am not curious enough to ask any more questions. I have enough to deal with these days.

David's solicitor has sent several messages in the past few weeks asking me to come to his office for a meeting. There had been a pleasant lull for some time and I thought that the hounding missives had come to an end but I was mistaken. I know what this is all about and I do not wish to acknowledge any requests from David, his solicitors, or any minions working on his behalf. I just want to be left alone and I don't understand why no one seems to respect that. I have offered as many pretexts as I can construct to avoid any confrontation with David, and I have no desire to yield to any of his recent demands. He has no legal standing and he is quite aware of this fact. I do not care how many solicitors he employs or how many messages he sends, I am not in a frame of mind to do his bidding. I know that somewhere inside my heart I still love him and care about his welfare but this love has faded into a subdued memory of a once vibrant feeling. Each day I strive to put the business of heartbreak behind me. Why will he not leave me in peace?

This morning's message was unsettling; it suggests that there will never come a time when I can finally close the door on that chapter of my life. *Mr. Livingston wishes to speak with you and will continue to pursue his goal despite your inattention to his requests. It is vital that you reply to this current appeal in this office on the 20th day of March or we will continue to pursue the matter by any means necessary to find an equitable solution.*

I have struggled to find my own equitable solution to this estrangement with David but avoidance as a solution has proven ineffective thus far. I have no wish to move backward, forward, or sideways, for it seems that movement in any direction on my part presages some sort of adverse consequence and it is only logical that avoidance of movement should affect an end to adversity or calamities in my life. Just stay in one spot, don't move, keep your head down, lie low, hold your breath, make no new decisions, encounter no one, and at all costs avoid unfamiliar situations, I keep reminding myself. Stay in the shadows of fate lest she cast her malevolent beams upon me once again. Each passing day, however, I find that it is increasingly difficult to stay hidden from my own life. Regularly charting my course to avoid the unexpected storms of misfortune, the boulders of opposition, the pitfalls of poor decisions, and the erratic crises of human encounters are proving to be quite unachievable in the occupation of life.

*Dear Sirs, I have no desire to meet in your office on the 20th of March or at any other time – not for any reason. Please advise your client that these enduring "pursuits" will continue to be met with resistance and will prove increasingly unsuccessful. Cease and desist in this act of harassment at once.*

*M. Barrington*

I need to send this out immediately. Ignoring their past missives has been futile, but now I hesitate because a response on my part may indicate a movement whose interpretation may be confused with compliance or progress. I do not wish to engage in *any* communications. I crumple the note and throw it into the bin. I just wish to be left alone.

# 12

## *Old Befana*

I never understood a great deal about God back in my day. Well, that's an understatement. Truth be told, I never took the time to understand such things because the choices around me were utterly confusing. Some of the things people did were downright creepy – like that augury business. Cut open an animal, have a peek at what they ate, how does it look when you pull out the guts – if the bowels look happy, everyone's happy. If not, you'd better look out. Seriously, if I ate some olives that went bad my bowels wouldn't look very happy either and neither would anyone whose job it is to dig around in there. But that's how it was back then; people were scared and looking in the oddest places for some good news. The general beliefs revolved around people trying to steer clear of some petty and vindictive gods that always seemed to be up to some kind of mischief, toying with people's affections, thwarting their hopes and dreams, and causing bedlam. I didn't get mixed up in that nonsense back then. The folks that had some extra money to live on used it to guarantee their fortunes and pad their lives with momentary comforts even though their appetites would change from one minute to the next. They wanted to keep the gods happy, the government happy, and the soldiers happy just so they could hang on to their *stuff*. Their allegiances seemed hell-bent on just about anything other than a relationship with a different kind of God because that God, as I later came to know, didn't concern himself with *stuff* – it was just stuff we used for living. So to them it didn't make any sense to revere someone who didn't care about stuff if they really cared about it

At the time, there were also some people who lived close to my village that seemed to have a relationship with a very special God, a one, true God they said, the one that didn't care about stuff; he seemed to care about *them*. That's what I'd heard; he'd do anything for them, anything at all, not like the crazy other gods that just messed around with people, but you had to be born into the line of people that belonged to that God, the one that cared about you. I wasn't born to that so I lived my life, woke up, worked, cleaned, ate, slept, and did it all over again each day. I didn't understand anything else.

It was *this* caring God who sent his Son into the world as a baby. For me, learning about the caring God's Son took a long time. I'm still learning. I must admit, I was secretly envious of people that belonged to a God that cared about them. I wanted God to care about me, too. Would it have been easier to dance along with the folks who tried to appease the scary gods? Maybe, but I didn't think so. I'll be honest, though, it wasn't easier going through life without any God at all. Sure, I didn't have to follow any special rules, or get caught up in some kind of a system, but it was sad for me to think that there was nothing great big out there that cared one way or the other what happened to me; that just wasn't a good feeling, it was rather an empty feeling. And the rules were a way to learn how to love the right way. But, I was a loner; I didn't have to please anyone, I just did what was right for the sake of it. Who was I that any great God should care about me? I lived my whole colorless life feeling like there wasn't much of a point to it all. I'd watched people die and they looked really annoyed that they had to leave their stuff where it was and other people would come along and take it. Very few people seemed to be happy to leave their stuff behind and get to the other side of the river. Something had to change. So when the opportunity came along some years later to get to know the love of a caring God it wasn't all that difficult to turn toward a new direction no matter what the cost. A young girl taught me about that a very long time ago.

Her name was Blandina and she was a servant girl, a slave actually, to a woman whose name escapes me right now. She was simple and sweet and fragile looking. Every day she would wake up, do the washing, fetch the water, make bread, feed her mistress, clean the stuff in the house and basically work her fingers down to nubs, and for what? Her existence didn't look much different than my own. It didn't seem to matter. People like little Blandina were regarded as inferior, repulsive, despicable. Her life had little value. *Stuff* would last longer than she would.

One day her mistress, maybe her name was Geneva, a beautiful and refined woman discovered some good news in the ideas of the people called Christians. You know, I really liked that lady Geneva. She was a kind mistress to Blandina and didn't abuse her. She was the sort of lady that did good things for people because she liked to, not because someone would take notice. But to most of the people in those days, what did it matter? If it benefited them personally to help people, wonderful, if not, they were considered soft and the world wasn't made for soft people. As far as most people were concerned her efforts amounted to nothing because there were always too many people who needed help and the task was futile, but somehow those in need did matter to her and her slave girl, Blandina. The young girl seemed to admire her mistress greatly and wished to be like her. When Geneva discovered Christianity Blandina was curious to learn more. They were both the sort of women that seemed right for this way of life. If I didn't know better, it seemed to me that they had found their purpose, not just in life, but in *being*. Their very act of living signified something and they realized it was significant beyond life itself. They learned this by listening to the messages that came from the Christians, the followers of the Son of the caring God.

The good news that this Son brought to us is that we *do* matter! The things we do matter. The things that happen to us matter, even if something bad happens to us and we don't deserve it, it matters to this God! It's not all for nothing or twisted up into the whims of childish gods and spun around for their amusement. Everything about our lives matters to this God because he cares about us whether we believe in him or not. The Son of this caring God, that Baby Jesus, was born a poor child, so poverty matters. He laughed and enjoyed the company of friends, went to weddings and dinner parties, and so joy matters. He cared about wounds, diseases, and torment, and so healing matters. He was betrayed, hurt, and abused, and thus suffering matters. Everything in life matters to this God that cares about us. I know; I could hardly believe it myself! This really was good news for all of us – every last one of us inferior, repulsive, and despicable nothings; we suddenly mattered in a way we never realized before.

I was pretty excited by this discovery. It seemed that I had more to gain from this association with Blandina than she did with me. She was a sweet and fragile girl, if she mattered to this caring God, then he mattered to her. They threatened her, told her to give up this nonsense and go back to revering the uncaring, devious, and immature gods that caused nothing but chaos or she would suffer. Honestly? The dear child would rather suffer because her suffering mattered to the caring God – it didn't matter to the creepy gods, they didn't give a fig for her suffering. She made a natural choice. She may have been "weak and unimportant" to the bullies that threatened her, but what she endured for God showed his strength and his importance; her suffering showed everyone the value of his love, and those that killed her lost so much more than they gained. Blandina was the first person I learned to miss and to grieve for, and I wanted to understand why she was willing to give herself to this God. It's a bigger-than-life caring that I learned from her. This encounter was a big leap for someone like me. I loaded these ideas into my satchel and carried them around with me. I'm happy to be reminded that I'm not as alone as I used to think.

# 13

## *Ivy*

With a small child around sleep is a thing of the past. Between maintaining this home for my mistress, taking care of Colleen during her illness, and giving Nolly the care a little one deserves, there is no time for rest. When I awaken each morning my eyes prickle with the duties of love. I burn a little extra kerosene during the night to do the washing and the cleaning, to bake some bread, and to prepare for the day's needs which amounts to doing all of my regular daytime chores during the nighttime hours while everyone is asleep. I don't mind, really, it's just that I have not had to work this hard since the rest of the staff resigned or were sent away. I take comfort in knowing that I'm not just serving someone else's family as I have in the past, I'm now of service to my own loved ones.

I came to this home when Mr. and Mrs. Barrington were still alive. Well, Mr. Barrington was old and feeble and I was brought on to help care for him in his last days. He had some type of sickness I'd never seen. The doctor called it a cancer of some type. The poor man had tumors the size of melons and there was nothing to be done. He suffered so and it pained young Miss Margaret to see her father in such torment. She seemed grateful for my presence. I brought up food for her dear father, helped to clean his wounds, and many times just sat and listened to him cry for no one else had the stomach for it. I stayed by his side until he took his last breath. When he lay dying Mrs. Barrington never left his side either; she held his hand and cried. Many visitors stopped by to pay their respects until finally the beloved man passed away. His wife and daughters kept vigil until the undertaker came to take him away. Within a year Mrs. Barrington joined her husband, though her passing came as a result of a carriage accident on her way to Glasgow to visit her sister, Meg. At that time Miss Margaret was overwrought. Losing both of her cherished parents in such a short time cast a spell of fragile unrest over the entire house. She had been engaged to Mr. Livingston and he had helped to divert her heart from grief to joy for quite some time. Eventually, they married and settled into a complicated union bound by a true but patchy sort of bond. As Mrs. Livingston, and heiress to the estate, she took over the entire business with the help of her husband and kept me on as her personal servant. It wasn't until much later when my mistress faced some insurmountable trials that the remainder of the household staff disappeared.

I tried to be of as much help as I could. As a result I've had some experience with illness, yes, but it is different when the malady attacks one's own beloved family as is the case now with Colleen. I have done my best, night and day, to nurse my sister back to health but her concern seems to be less with her own recovery and more with the nurturing of her child. When I ask what I might bring her to eat, she responds with *bring Nolly a bit of soup*. When I ask if she is comfortable, if she needs another blanket or pillow, she tells me to play with the child. She has abdicated her needs for the needs of her child. Does she not realize that the primary need in a child's life is a healthy mother? I have told her this. She tells me she will be fine. I do not believe her; she grows weaker each day even though I have brought her to a warm and comfortable home. She is languishing. During brief moments of strength, she holds Nolly close to her and talks about special people and places, about heaven and angels, and the very special grace we get when we need it the most. Nolly nods her head and lays her head upon her mother's shoulder, sometimes stroking her mother's face with her tiny hands.

Sometimes, Nolly sits for hours by her mother's side, chatting to herself and playing with the ragdoll. She seems reluctant to leave the room lest her mother vanish in her absence. When Colleen sleeps I am able to persuade Nolly to come with me to another room, to play with some blocks of wood in the kitchen while I prepare dinner, to assemble a puzzle of shapes while I dust the study in my mistress's absence, so that she is able to enjoy a sense of freedom once in a while. Today in the study she has spotted the figurine of the old woman sitting on the lampstand near the bookcase.

"What is this?" she asks.

"It is a statue," I reply.

"Why is it here with all these other statues?" she wants to know. "This one is different."

I have no idea, but I answer, "My mistress likes this statue." Nolly looks at the statuette and then at me with a look of incredulity. Who would like this ugly statue, her furrowed brows seem to ask. I continue to attend to my duties while Nolly studies the old woman and forces her to hop around the lampstand. Suddenly, she puts the statue down and laughs. I haven't heard Nolly laugh in all the weeks she has lived under this roof.

"Can I take this statue to my room to show Mommy?" she asks.

"I don't think so, my sweet. My mistress is quite fond of this statue and she will be very cross if she does not find it exactly where she left it."

"But can't we borrow it for a few minutes? We can bring her right back before your mistress comes home and put her exactly in the same spot. Mommy would like to see this funny thing. It will make her smile, I think. Please?"

Nolly hasn't asked me for one thing since the day she arrived. She has been no trouble at all and she is very obedient and quiet. How can I possibly refuse her this one favor?

"We must return her immediately," I tell her. She casts me a conspiratorial smile.

# 14

## *Margaret*

Today, Mr. Trumble, the bank bursar, is giving me the oddest look when I present myself at his window. I have done business here, with him directly, for many years but for some time now he looks at me as one would regard a leper. His eyes narrow as if he is peering cautiously at the inside of a wound. But he remains strictly polite. I think he believes that the only thing that separates me from a complete recluse is that I make regular visits to the Queen's Bank to withdraw funds for living expenses and to transfer funds for business dealings. How I conduct my life once I leave the confines of her majesty's reserve is my business and mine alone.

"Good day, Mrs. Livingston."

"Good day, Mr. Trumble. The usual withdrawal, please, and a statement of my accounts."

"Yes, Ma'am."

As I turn around I spy the elder Rodgers brother by the front entrance, one of David's solicitors. Am I being followed, I wonder? I'd hate to think I'm becoming paranoid on top of everything else, but he seems to be staring directly at me and heading toward me. I am tempted to bolt out of the bank without completing my business transaction but this would most likely result in even stranger reactions from Mr. Trumble on my future visits.

For the moment Mr. Rodgers seems to be keeping his distance but his eyes remain focused on me lest he lose sight of me. I take my bank notes and account records as graciously as I can from Mr. Trumble's hand and walk briskly toward the door, not nearly fast enough, however.

"Mrs. Livingston, a word, please ..." Mr. Rodgers stands between me and the door, but in a low voice I warn him, "Stand aside, Mr. Rodgers if you do not wish for me to create a scene. This is neither the time, nor the place."

"We have requested a separate time and place to meet but you fail to respond."

"My lack of response *is* my response, Mr. Rodgers. I have no wish to meet, nor do I have anything to say. Now stand aside before I alert the officer that I am being harassed." At that he takes only one step to the side as I try to get past him.

"Mr. Livingston only wishes to be heard..."

"Which conflicts with my wish to be left alone. If you continue to badger me, stalk me, or otherwise contact me, I shall be forced to..."

"But, Mrs. Livingston, this needs to be resolved."

I turn around again to walk back toward the bursar's window. Mr. Rodgers lets out an audible sigh and leaves the bank. I feign an act of organizing my belongings at a nearby counter until I feel it is safe to leave the premises but first I return to Mr. Trumble's window.

"What can I do for you Mrs. Livingston?"

"Yes, Mr. Trumble, I'd quite forgotten that I should require some additional funds. I shall be away for a while."

"Yes, Mrs. Livingston. All is well, I hope?"

I do not reply. I take my additional funds and hail the first carriage nearby. I've no wish to encounter any more solicitors on my way home. My mind is made up. I will leave London sooner than I'd planned and take the first train to Grange-Over-Sands to spend some time at my seaside home, alone and in peace. Dear God, what must one do to be left in the peace of solitude?

# 15

## *Ivy*

I have no idea what has caused my mistress to leave so suddenly for the seaside. She left so quickly she had no time to notice that Nolly and I had failed to return the statuette to its post on the lampstand as yet. It's my fault. We'd taken it to Colleen because Nolly had insisted that her mother would be delighted to see such an unsightly bauble. Colleen opened her eyes, took one look at the little haggardly figurine and laughed herself into a fitful cough. Nolly was so pleased to have received such a response that she persisted in animating the figurine to achieve additional responses.

"What is it?" Colleen asked when she had recovered.

"I do not know," I answered. "My mistress is quite fond of it, however. She brought it home from a jumble sale one day and she pays it more attention than anything else in this home."

"Did she buy all the statues in his house," Nolly asked. Colleen had become tired and once again fallen asleep. I took Nolly over by the fireplace and sat her on my lap. She clutched the figurine tightly in her small hands.

"No, my sweet, my mistress inherited this home and everything in it. She has bought very little that you see lying about."

"It is your job to remove the dust from all the things lying about." I watched as she stroked her finger over the statue. Tenderly, she caressed the face almost as if her touch could

57

smooth away the wrinkles of age and coax a smile from the wood. "Would your mistress be angry if I wanted to keep this?"

"Yes, dearest, she would be upset. She loves this little statue. It is not ours to keep. Why do you want such an ugly thing when you have a smiling little doll to play with?"

Nolly shot me a disapproving look. "She is not ugly, Auntie Ivy. She reminds me of a granny. I do not have a granny. I think grannies bring sweets to their grandchildren when they are good." She turned the figure around – "See! She is carrying a knapsack, and I think it is full of treats."

"Well, you may be right about that," I answered. "How about if we put her away and you and I will go into the kitchen and make some real treats together. We'll let your mommy rest a while and maybe when she wakes up she would enjoy some of our treats, yes?"

Nolly nodded her head. "Can we bring granny to the kitchen with us? I think she would like to watch us. She likes baking treats for children and she will make sure we do this right." I smiled at my niece's imagination. It is always a marvel how children are so adept at governing their senses through the heart.

The kitchen is brightly lit at this time of day. The windows near the wash basin invite the afternoon sun into the room and fill it with life. Normally, this functional room has a somber effect for I enter it only with an eye for chores. How is it that a child can bring so much vitality to the ordinary? Together we assemble the ingredients we need on the long wooden table in the kitchen. Nolly stands on a caned chair and rolls up her sleeves. Her job is to mix the cocoa powder with the butter. When she tires I add the sugar and mix them together.

"Can I add the eggs?" she asks. After she adds the first egg and we fish out the bits of broken shell I add the remaining eggs and a bit more cocoa powder. Nolly adds two handfuls of almonds. "Granny said to add a pinch of hot pepper powder to give this a better flavor," Nolly says. What an odd ingredient to suggest. We add just a tiny pinch to the cookie mixture. When they are finished baking we find them to be remarkably tasty. Nolly pretends to feed a crumb of cookie to "granny."

"Does she like our cookies?" I ask. Nolly shakes her head. "It needs more pepper."

# 16

## *Old Befana*

Gattud was once chased by a wolf all through town, in and out of gardens, past the orchards, and finally deep into the grotto where she'd hidden between two large boulders near the top of the cave. She had wedged herself in so high up and out of reach that the wolf gave up and left without its morning meal. Gattud, however, had lodged herself in rather tightly and was stuck for most of the day, meowing and lamenting her predicament. She was always pretty good at escaping a bad fate and I've been around long enough to know that she certainly outlived the mythical nine lives. She was a loner and she liked it that way. I think she even managed to escape the occasional romance with a lascivious tom for I never saw her give off a litter. We were simpatico, she and I. I'm sure she dropped in on other houses but she seemed to think my house was her provincial seat. Of course I'd feed her and give her a bit of milk if I had any; she'd curl up in my window, the one that faced east and soak in the morning sunshine. That was my visiting friend, Gattud, and I've never forgotten her warmth and affection. She was the only living thing to have ever claimed me. She wouldn't let any other cats near me. I belonged to her alone. Goodness, I think the child in this house reminds me of my old Gattud.

This little girl hovers over me no matter where I've been set down. She'll pick me up, put nonsense words into my mouth and force me to frolic in every room of the house. Once, she even put me on top of the bronze horse that stands in the entryway. I was sure I was going to fall and break in two or get another unsightly dent. Granny, indeed. Well, I'm sure if I had ever had the chance to enjoy a child of my own or a grandchild, I wouldn't have minded one like this little sprite. She is no bother to anyone and amuses herself quite well while her poor mother strives to get healthier and her overworked auntie does the job of the entire household staff that used to take care of this place. The child never complains that she's left alone so much but when she does manage to warrant someone's attention, she loves nothing better than listening to stories. Her mother is too ill to indulge her these days and poor Ivy is unaccustomed to children, but she's learning. On this particular day, her auntie came down from the attic with a dusty old children's book. Many things had been put away over the years and this book, for some reason, ended up in storage instead of on a proper shelf in the study.

The child settled into her auntie's lap and clutched me tightly so that I could face the book and listen to the story, too. Ivy began reading, "Nowhere in all of Grayson village could a rabbit be found. Where once there were hundreds of rabbits roaming the village and eating the cabbages, flowers, beet sprouts, and apples, now there was only a fat cat and a mangy dog that kept all the rabbits out of the village and away from the precious gardens. The rabbits spent their days hiding on the other side of Heartland Hill and feeding on tiresome thistle weed. Heartland wasn't really a hill; it was more of a bump in the meadow but the villagers had given the bump a name because it was known at times to thump from within and all the townsfolk thought that it sounded like a heartbeat. They made up a story that a giant was buried beneath it and he would gobble up children if they tried to cross his bulging hill. So, the children stayed on one side of Heartland Hill and the rabbits stayed on the other. Until one day little Maggie Carey spotted a courageous little rabbit trying to cross over the hill to get to some fresh new cabbages. Maggie was rather brave as well and did not fear the sleeping giant. She wanted to play with the rabbit..."

Within minutes the poor tired auntie had fallen asleep in mid-sentence. Nolly looked up at her weary aunt and asked me if I could continue telling her the story. What did I know about this story? I didn't even know how to read, so I made things up as I went along about how two unlikely characters can become the very best of friends. At the end, the little girl *kissed me.*

# 17

## *Margaret*

Three weeks into my self-imposed exile and I can finally begin to feel the troubles at home melting away. In Grange, there is no fear other than what I bring with me. I have been chanting an intonation of various phrases every time an unwanted thought creeps into my head. *Give thy thoughts no tongue... Expectation is the root of all heartache... Some rise by sin, and some by virtue fall...* I must give credit to the brilliance of Mr. Shakespeare for without his words my own would only serve as shovels to dig my grave. This time away from Chestnut Hill must provide some perspective; I do wish to regain some foothold on my life but the memories that haunt me and the fears that lurk around every shadow of my home make it impossible for me to step outside of my own mind and see the situation with the clarity of intelligence rather than the murkiness of emotion.

What I love most about Grange-over-Sands are the decorated borders of privacy; each home is its own little retreat and each garden a haven of creativity. The first of spring's splendor adds a splash of yellows and violets to my morning stroll; the pansies and daffodils are poking their frilly heads through the hardened earth in spite of the cool temperatures. It is a pleasure to walk the quiet neighborhoods without the bustle of wily townsfolk pushing past me to get to work. I can breathe in Grange; I can feel the tension in my neck give way to relief. Grange has all the ingredients necessary for an illusion of peace. In the public gardens there is a large kidney-shaped pond that invites the local wildlife to pierce through the stillness of the picture-perfect landscape with tweets and squawks and wails of buoyancy. On the benches that surround the pond there are the occasional elderly residents who enjoy bird-feeding at daybreak. It is a gentle place to sit and think.

The first order of business: David's persistent aspirations must be dealt with in a way that puts things at rest permanently. I cannot allow these annoying interruptions to continue. I must decide what to do: should I talk to him knowing that he will persist in defending his pervasive needs of the moment without regard for my feelings or should I find legal redress to satisfy my need for well-being? I am not fit to enter into one more verbal debate about the powerlessness of our present circumstances. Neither of us could prevent the rapid decline of our dreams; it seemed that together we were twice as weak not twice as strong. We needed something that proved to be missing in our marriage. Our affection for one another was not enough. If the situation cannot be resolved, then I suppose prudence demands that it should be dissolved.

Secondly: Because I have limited David's access to the family business, some of the accounts and affairs have been neglected for a time and I need someone I can trust to oversee them. Though David and I used to work well together, I now find that running the entire enterprise alone is quite taxing. I recognize that the limitations on his position must compel his demands to meet with me on occasion but this is out of the question. David has such a talent for analyzing matters; to him everything is black and white which works well for business matters but a marriage must take in an array of colors and depth. Of course, I could just do what father suggested in his final days – sell the business and invest in something I find meaningful.

Thirdly: And I'm not even certain if this is something with which I need to concern myself, but Ivy's issues with her sister must find a resolution. I just don't want Ivy to be overburdened. She has been invaluable to me as a housekeeper and assistant. Hopefully, by the time I return the woman will have recovered and she and the child can find new circumstances. Though I have seen and heard nothing from these guests in my home it seems that the idea that there are others in the house that can neither be seen nor heard creates some type of ghostly presence with which I am uncomfortable.

Here in Grange I can utilize the clarity of thinking that is needed to consider my options with the knowledge that there is no rush to do so. I can enjoy the absence of urgency. There are memories here that are as calming as the kneading waves of Morecombe Bay. Since childhood I found that walking along the strand freed my mind from the complexities of life. It is so easy to lose myself in simplicity. This morning there are pink-footed geese flying overhead to rest in the fields nearby. There is nothing to do here but untangle my mind by focusing on a few sandpipers that skitter rapidly toward and away from the water, inviting one into equally careless folly. Chestnut Hill offers no such opportunity for abandonment. Here it is safe to forsake my tightly fortified life among these unrestrained creatures.

## 18

### *Ivy*

Colleen is five years my junior and when I left Wicklow to come to England and go into service for the Barrington family she was merely a child of nine. My brothers were still at home: Killian who worked the farm, Aidan who was next in line after me, and Tim who was friends with Danny Doyle. Danny was a bit of a ruffian, just like my brothers, they were always getting into scrapes and shenanigans but nothing illegal, just the kind of things that boys do. The three of them were known as the troublesome trio ever since the time they disassembled old man Murphy's chicken coop that was built on the west side of his house and rebuilt it on the east side. They leveled the dirt so that there was no trace that the coop had been there and moved the chickens into their new location. They did this all during the night. In the morning poor old Murphy came out of his house and took the usual left turn to get some eggs from his chickens. He started cursing at the top of his lungs. "Where's me chickens? I'll get the bog-jumpers that stole me chickens. Wait till I get me shotgun and kill them swine that run off with me chickens. Oh, me poor chickens." Murphy ran around his patch screaming for his chickens, even after he saw that they were on the other side of the house. Those couldn't possibly be *his* chickens.

It was a few months before anyone found out that it was the trio that played the trick. It was Tim, my younger brother that couldn't help bragging about it to his other friend Sean, who told Quinn, who told his sister Aishling, who told Fr. Dooley, the priest at St. Anne's, who then scolded the boys and told the parents. My father's response was to make the boys rebuild the coop on the west side of the house but not before going out to the barn and having a good laugh about it. Danny Doyle who only lived with his Ma went without what would have been a meager supper. That was only the beginning – no matter how many scoldings, trips to the shed, or missed meals of potatoes and lard, the boys were undaunted. And when they grew older, they went off to the north to join the fight to regain what Ireland lost to England many generations ago. Only Danny returned. He wasn't the same again; he missed his friends; he missed the adventures, and he found comfort in a sweet lass, our younger sister named Colleen, and he married her. I do believe Danny loved my sister but he didn't want his life to change. He wanted it all, my brothers, the trouble, the escapades, and a pretty wife to come home to. Isn't that the way of it? When Nollaig was born Danny understood he should take care of his little family and even though he despised the English he brought them here when he found work in a candle factory near Cotswold. But he'd had no example of tenacity since his father had left him and his Ma when he was not much more than six. So Danny bolted just a few short months after Nolly's second birthday. That was just two years ago. Colleen had always been a rather delicate sort and tried her best to work to make ends meet. She was devoted to prayer but didn't understand the need to be open to inspiration. It was as if she prayed with her hands over her ears! But, who am I to talk? I stopped praying long ago and I've probably forgotten how. From time to time I've thought about talking to God, but instead I forge ahead with all the things I have to take care of in my life. At this moment I find myself thinking about asking if God can please help Colleen. I feel ashamed to ask for something after so many years of not talking to him. My sister has been through so much. She ended up in the women's workhouse and had to work night and day for a bit of food for herself and Nolly until she became too ill to continue.

I never really had the chance to know my sister very well. I suppose I've been too busy trying to manage my own life, working hard, and taking care of Mrs. Livingston. I never went back to Wicklow, not even when I'd heard that my Ma and Pa had died of the cholera. I cried and I cried, and I paid two shillings for a Mass at St. Bart's, but I was so cut off from my family for so long, I think I was grieving more for the time I'd lost with them since I'd left home at such a young age to find work. I'd promised myself I didn't want to be without a home or food and for some reason for the past fifteen years, that's all that's mattered. Until now.

# 19

## *Old Befana*

*"May God give you, for every storm, a rainbow,*
*For every tear, a smile,*
*For every care, a promise,*
*And a blessing in each trial.*
*For every problem life sends, a faithful friend to share*
*For every sigh, a sweet song,*
*And an answer for each prayer." ~ An Irish prayer*

On this quiet morning I'm being held on the child's lap keeping vigil with her at her mother's side. The young woman's breathing is quite labored and her limbs are twitching from time to time. When she gasps for breath the child runs her hand over her mother's forehead. Ivy is out taking care of business for her absent mistress and the child seems just as tranquil when someone is at home as she is when someone is not. She appears to monitor her own behavior as if her mother is watching over her rather than the other way around; but for comfort I believe she clutches me tightly and speaks as if she can hear me reply.

It can prick the thickest skin to watch a young child enter the world of loss. Nolly continues to talk rapidly without the need to take the occasional breath, whether it is simple chatter, or made up stories, she is trying to keep her mother here. The child's noises are a constant drone to hold off the fear of silence. To love is to learn about being afraid, but for love to ripen there must be no fear. Nolly does not want her small world to become even smaller.

When the sun's rays enter the room through the narrow window next to the bed it comes in stealthily like a cloaked phantom sneaking into a private place where unspoken hopes can no longer remain hidden. Nolly has taken something from her mother's hands and without pause she begins to instruct me about the importance of this delicate chain of wooden beads. She tells me that the beads are a way to talk to a mother in heaven and to think about God. That's what her mother had taught her. She holds them firmly as if she has pried a treasure away from a small sanctuary. "These are what we use to say the Ayle Mary many times," she says. "The Ayle Mary is very special, Mommy says, because she's a mommy too. So when we talk to the Ayle Mary we say her name like the angel said it. And then the angel tells her she has somebody very important in here." She pokes me in my wooden belly and continues. "And the important baby is called Jesus. And he is okay in her tummy because there is fruit in her 'woom.'" Nolly pauses for a moment. "He is the baby that God put in there and the Baby Jesus is okay inside his Mommy." Again the child pauses then continues. "My Mommy says that when I get older I can have 'comunin' and then I can have the Baby Jesus in here, too." Again with the poking. "I have to be very careful to keep him in here just like the Ayle Mary because Mommy says I have to want him. If I want too many other things then there won't be room for him and I have to get rid of other things. But I don't have any other things, just my Mommy, and my auntie and a little granny."

Sometimes it is just a soft wordless presence that provides comfort for someone who needs us. The child fingers the beads as she prays looking back and forth between the rosary and her mother. The woman's breathing becomes shallow. She seems more serene than she has in days. When her breathing finally stops, the child stares intently into her mother's face.

She pokes her mother's cheek as if to prompt her to breathe again but the stillness is tangible. "I think Mommy has gone to be with the Ayle Mary now." The child grips me tighter than ever and together we sit in silence, the kind of silence that's necessary to hear a fluttering spirit.

# 20

## *Ivy*

It doesn't feel real somehow; was Colleen ever here? Was she ever really a part of my life? I tried to do all I could for her. The doctor said her illness had progressed beyond the point where she could be helped. At the hospital they may have been able to prolong her life by weeks only, but she would not be with her child or in the comfort of a home when the time came, and inevitably it would come. Nolly never kept her mother out of ear's reach in those last few days. The child seemed to know that her mother was slipping away. I feel dreadful that I was not here with them when it finally happened. The poor little thing was left alone with Colleen when she passed. There have been many times in my life when I wished that I could divide myself in two and attend to multiple things at one time but never more than in this case. I'd only been to the post office to take care of some business and when I returned Nolly met me at the door with the news.

"Mommy stopped hurting," Nolly had told me. Those were the last words she spoke for over a week. She has been keeping her own silent bereavement ritual. I've asked her several times if she wants to talk about her Mommy but she always shakes her head quietly. If I didn't know any better, I would say she looks like she's trying very hard to keep a secret, as if she knows something that I do not. I'm worried about her but she doesn't entrust me with her feelings. It's as if the poor child has wandered into a woeful garden looking for stepping stones that lead to the painless world where her mother has gone; it would be very easy for her to get tangled in a thicket of sorrow; it has happened many times before around this house. Here, fear and sorrow live together like members of the family, those members who must be obeyed. Yet, despite our lack of confidences, Nolly and I have settled into a genuine routine that seems to work for both of us. Instead of confiding in me she whispers into the ears of the small, decrepit statue that she carries around night and day.

Each morning upon rising, Nolly insists on praying her little version of the rosary which basically involves repeating the name of the Virgin Mary as her mother taught her, complete with Irish brogue. We have a swift meal of biscuits and fresh milk with a touch of coffee and sugar and then our day begins. Nolly has the task of shining. That is what she calls dusting. Her first task of the day is shining anything within reach. God love this precious child. At first she did her chores quietly, but after a few weeks she has begun to sing and chatter as she shines the world around her. I have noticed, however that she demands that she wears one of my aprons so that she can keep the *granny* in her pocket. She seems comforted by granny's presence. The apron's pockets are deep, she tells me, and granny won't fall out while she shines. Her conversations with granny are quite mysterious. Of course, to me, they seem one-sided, but certainly to Nolly there is a mutual exchange in place. It was the day that granny taught her a song that I truly began to wonder.

> *From starry skies descending,*
> *Thou comest, glorious King,*
> *A manger low Thy bed,*
> *In winter's icy sting;*
> *O my dearest Child most holy,*
> *Shudd'ring, trembling in the cold!*
> *Great God, Thou lovest me!*
> *What suff'ring Thou didst bear,*
> *That I near Thee might be!*

It seemed too clear, too complete, to be a child's song of fancy. It had all the undertones of an ancient form of devotion. It sounded like a real song, not something strung together in the mind of a four year-old. The melody repeated consistently and the words of the song were passionate and true. It did not sound like any Irish song that Colleen may have taught her and Nolly hasn't left my side to learn anything from someone new. It sounded very much like a Christmas song and we were still months away from the Christmas holidays. Nolly was singing the song several times a day and finally the enigma of this song had gotten the best of my curiosity.

"Nolly, love, where did you learn that song?

Quite matter-of-factly she answered, "Granny taught me. It's the only song she knows." Of course I remained quiet wondering if Colleen's death had damaged the child. Was her imagination crossing an invisible line into a place from which she may not be able to return? For lack of anything better to say I repeated her words in question form, "Granny taught you? It's the only song she knows?"

Nolly nodded her head. "Yes, at first she sang it funny."

"Funny?"

"Yes, Auntie, funny words I didn't understand."

"You didn't understand?" I was beginning to feel like one of those birds that I've heard about that mock the language of humans. Even Nolly seemed to notice my lack of sensibility.

"All right, Nolly, tell me about the song and how you learned it."

"It's a song about the Baby Jesus that was born and he was poor and he was cold and he was God. Granny was singing it and I tried to sing it too and then I learned it."

"It sounds very much like a Christmas song. Is it a Christmas song?"

"Well, granny says if you love the Baby Jesus then it is Christmas all the time."

"How does granny know about the Baby Jesus?"

"Oh, well, she said she heard a story about him when he was born and now she cares about him very much. She's been trying to find him. She has a present for him and she always gives it to children she finds just in case it's the Baby Jesus. I told her I'm not the Baby Jesus. I'm not a baby. She laughed. She knows that but she said she sees his face in the smiles of little children like me."

I felt too astonished to respond to this discourse. I told Nolly to keep singing the song because it is very beautiful. She sings it like there is a buried joy that has bubbled up through her recent wounds and she can sing her way back to the childhood she knew before.

We continued throughout our day of caring for the house and making little meals for the two of us. One of Nolly's afternoon activities is to go outside in the trellised area behind the house and get some fresh air. She "gardens" by pulling up the naughty flowers that grow where they are not supposed to and she replants them in a bin full of dirt. By the time she has completed this small task she is delighted and fatigued. Sometimes she even makes me small chocolate biscuits with the dirt from the garden and I sit with her in the late afternoon. We have tea and I pretend to eat her biscuits. She shakes her head no and then asks if we can have real biscuits.

By the time we crawl into our beds at night, she is exhausted, and for some reason I feel invigorated. She no longer sleeps in the room she shared with her mother. I have set up a cot for Nolly in my room next to the kitchen. Granny sleeps on the nightstand between us, wrapped in a soft mantle of promise.

# 21

## *Old Befana*

Some of my visits have been puzzling – like the time I spent with a group of children in a place across the sea from my hometown, a place called Zillah. Mother in Heaven it was hot! Every day the temperatures were harsh enough to melt lightning right out of the sky. The streets and villages were as dry and deserted as burial grounds. And to complete the picture the usual birds that squatted in the area were huge, bald, with an evil look in their eyes. They sat still, waiting for something to stop moving. Creepy looking creatures, but the group of children I was visiting seemed to make sport of throwing rocks at those griffons and then running to hide behind some nearby boulders in case they should provoke a response.

One day, the youngest in the group, Ajeeb, usually disliked by his companions because of his hostile personality, earned their fearful admiration by hitting his target griffon dead-center while the spooky old bird was busily nibbling on a juicy fennec. The disturbance was not appreciated by the bird and it took off in the direction of little Ajeeb and was primed to attack when the child tripped in a trench and fell. The griffon was on top of him in nothing flat. The rest of the children, all hiding behind boulders didn't notice that their playmate was in trouble until it was almost too late. When the oldest child, Mohy, saw what had happened he shrieked out a sort of tribal wail and all the children followed suit, running with rocks toward the bird and screeching at the top of their lungs. The bird went back to his fennec but poor Ajeeb was worse for the wear. He was unconscious, mainly from fear, and had a few bites taken out of the flesh on his back. Mohy picked him up and carried him back to the refuge beneath the ruins of an ancient amphitheater built by the Romans long, long ago. This is where this abandoned group of children lived and cared for each other. I watched the determined way in which they tended to Ajeeb's wounds with a brine mixture and a few dirty rags. Their care for one another seemed more rooted in pity than in love. They did not know how to love for they hardly remembered receiving it, but they had an innate sense of human dignity that dominated their interactions. They were cast-offs from nomadic clusters and they wore as their tribal badge a primitive motive to ensure that their little clan survived. Each child brought a special character to the effort. Mohy was the oldest, the strong leader-type but he wore a look of pride that discouraged any charity. No one could offer him anything that he could not acquire on his own. His pride was costly and could not be bought at any kindly price. He and his brother Marid shared one ego between them. Mohy stole from people who were stingy and Marid stole from the charitable folks. This ensured that they would steal from those who refused to share and also to steal one's ability to share. They decided that this was the best way to have power, just like the government under which they lived.

As for young Ajeeb he hadn't been abandoned by his people, he'd escaped them. Always a rather difficult child he had suffered terrible abuse at the hands of his father and uncles which left him with feelings of mistrust for people and the world around him; he was consumed with hatred and anger. His ability to hit the griffon with such precision was the result of persistent practice. Somewhere deep inside it was his goal to destroy people. He wanted some kind of justice.

For the most part the faults of these children grew not out of a desire for evil but an unrequited desire for good. Good was only what they created for themselves, but they were unable to afford the commodity of trust. They'd learned to guard their own backs even if it meant guarding the back of the person standing next to you. These children may have once known love but love had been the worst of traitors. In their world, an absence of love had allowed hostility, skepticism, and short-sightedness to grow freely. They lived with an acknowledged fear that no one really cared about them. My presence was a mystery to me. I didn't see how I could help.

How I came to be in that place had much to do with the curiosity of a solitary world traveler, poor planning, starvation, and the remnants in his backpack. It was a girl in the little group named Mimi who found me after the griffons had finished with the traveler for they had no use for the contents of his travel bag. She gave me the name Bada` which I understood meant that I was out in the open again after being concealed. Seems reasonable. I've been called some unusual names in my travels but it never really mattered. Who I am has more to do with what I do rather than what someone calls me. Mimi took me back to the camp and showed me to her wounded companion, Ajeeb. That is how I came to be with this group, but Ajeeb in particular.

This unusual group of children managed their little settlement beneath the ruins quite well without the aid of adults. When they weren't taunting vultures, they worked by taking turns tending the small herds of goats and sheep of local farmers. Some of them exchanged their services for food. Left behind by some Bedouins, these children became self-sufficient and always took in other abandoned children. It was an independent cooperative and my presence hardly seemed necessary which is what made it so puzzling. On the day Ajeeb was attacked by the griffon Mimi felt he needed a healing Bada` at his side. The wounds from the griffon weren't nearly as deep as the wounds he'd suffered at the hands of his family. When Mimi entered the alcove and brought me to Ajeeb, his anger and fear had peaked. He grabbed a nearby rock and struck her on the head causing her to collapse at his side. Mimi was badly hurt but Ajeeb was too stunned at what he'd done to push her away. She put her arm around him and a steady flow of blood and tears drenched his shoulder. She kept repeating, "It's okay, Ajeeb, it's okay." For the rest of the day and into the next I was wedged between these two wounded children who lay weeping together, each for different reasons. Mimi cried for her friend until she passed into the next life, and Ajeeb cried himself into a new resolve. What he'd always believed he wanted, to hurt someone, was fatefully disappointing. This new experience of sympathy, an unexpected closeness of shared sorrow, was the feeling that seared the spirit within him and changed him.

I remained Ajeeb's healing Bada`, a reminder of his friend Mimi, until the day he died in London many decades later after spending his career as a photo journalist. His camera was his livelihood; his talent was in targeting keen moments. Of course, his very first camera he'd stolen from a group of pilgrims traveling east. Over the years I encouraged him to focus his lens on his living companions. He started taking pictures of the children in his clan. He'd captured many pictures of these orphaned children and as he grew older the pictures attracted the attention of a foreign magazine. Later, it was his undaunted readiness to travel into risky areas and his perceptive eye for recognizing the soul of need that helped him to earn the reputation of a journalist who knew how to expose the best and the worst in humanity. He grew to be a very successful man who covered many important stories, mostly about abused, neglected or starving children, especially in the Middle East and North Africa. He won a big prize for exposing a group of human traffickers who were selling children into adult trades. He taught the world to care about children living in fear. I was proud of him like he was my own kid. If you can help one child to turn hardship into something good you can save a huge chunk of the future.

But I can't take credit for when things turn out well; the real pat on the back goes to the one who helps me, shows me where I need to be and what I need to do. I'm not being silly here – it's true. A human breath is unremarkable and unseen; and yet if it is expelled through a musical instrument it can, in some cases, produce a sound that hails from heaven. I'm telling you, it's amazing how this wonderful caring God can work through anyone, even the unbelievers! The one who is good accomplishes good. By discovering the kindness of God I've been a more useful Befana. I had an awful lot to learn about caring for others. If it were up to me alone I'd still be hiding in my little life and wishing things were different.

# 22

## *Margaret*

Grange-Over-Sands has that mystical, tucked-away quality about it that is both inviting and withdrawn. Once you alight from the train and take the coach into Braithwaite you feel like you've left behind the incessant titter-tatter of expectations that pick at your life which leave you feeling consumed rather than whole. Here, I can put on the marginalized cloak of a refugee and blend into the shadows. Since I don't really belong here full time there are no expectations.

My house on Eden Mews no longer has a clear view of Morecambe Bay ever since the town built the Raven's Nest Hotel on the street below. What I love most about this house is its character of sheer willfulness, if such a thing is possible for a house that is more than ninety years old. Its balkiness stems from a peculiar ability to blend into the landscape like a mound of sandstone stationed in the desert. And yet it stands out among its neighbors as well. While the new houses in Grange decorate the hills along the bay with an array of maroon bricks or a newly minted assortment of Victorian pastels plucked right out of an Easter bonnet, my Eden Mews home sports an exterior jacket the color of flint so that on overcast days it stands invisible behind a curtain of mist. It is the bold, eclectic architecture that startles the unsuspecting passersby with its mad shapes and angles. What a sight! It has the effect of either drawing perplexing stares or being disregarded as an anomaly that the mind cannot interpret. The old house reflects the eccentric personality of my grandfather, Duncan Stewart, my mother's father who'd imported granite, limestone and slate from Scotland to have this awkward house built on a hill near the sea. My mother, Roslyn, the youngest and only surviving child of ten siblings inherited the house at age fifteen when Grandfather Duncan died in a squall at sea. The anatomy of this house has always reminded me of a child's mishap with building blocks, a hodgepodge of ecclesial and military styles – but that was my grandfather, always chasing peace and war in the same direction.

When I was a child my parents would bring the three of us girls to this seaside home for several weeks in the summer. My father would then return to London to tend to business affairs but my mother relished the time that she could spend with us unfettered by urban cares. My sister Mary had her summer friends as well and later on a few young men to amuse her, but Anne was actively on the prowl for recreation and any shops she could find for she felt lost without the more plentiful retailers back home. I, however, was always content to sit on the second story balcony, that odd protrusion that looked like an urn resting outside the music room and take comfort in reading something by Wordsworth, Austen, or the very latest by G.M. Hopkins.

*"Nothing is so beautiful as spring - when weeds, in wheels, shoot long and lovely and lush; Thrush's eggs look little low heavens, and thrush through the echoing timber does so rinse and wring the ear, it strikes like lightning to hear him sing."* Hopkins' melodic words still ring in my ears.

Since arriving here last month I have not picked up my old favorites from the bookshelf and disappointingly this spring has been too cold and wet for me to enjoy the luxury of sitting on the balcony at all. My small grace is that I don't have to deal with anyone that wishes to engage in conversation. I am content at the moment with the delivery of *The London Times* so that I can read about being at home without actually being present. Perusing the society pages allows me to keep up with old acquaintances without having to feel the cold air of pity brush against my open wounds. I don't have to attend social functions to learn all about my former friends. Today, the *Times* report that our old friends Robert and Stasia Cummingsworth hosted a fabulous party at their home in Kensington last week and that it was attended by the ambassador from South Africa. It's not necessary to participate in gossip to find out who attended the party, what they were wearing, and who appeared with a notable dignitary on her arm. I enjoy being aware of what everyone is doing without having to participate in the events. I no longer blend in with this lifestyle by my own choice. I never really enjoyed taking part in the social strata with its endless obligations, not the way David did. He thrived on parties, soirees, hunting weekends, polo matches, the whole *look at me, I am wealthy, see what I have and what I do* scenario. I was bored with that life when I'd met him but seeing it through his eyes gave it a renewed albeit short-lived sparkle. He knew how to *enjoy* that life. I knew how to cope with it. I'd known from the start it wasn't so much my father's fortune that attracted him, it was the excitement that attracted him. His family had made their fortunes as diamond merchants, but a series of bad decisions and the natural decline of legacies over several generations had diminished the bequests once David was born. His father, Arthur Livingston, along with his brothers and cousins, maintained an opulent lifestyle based on bank credits which soon defaulted. David was a good and honest businessman and he had always claimed that wealth didn't matter unless one could still enjoy life without it. I wanted something from life I could not put into words. Who knows, had I been born a peasant I might have been happier but the silver spoon lodged in my mouth tasted of bitter opulence that masked any flavor of sweet simplicity. I have all that money can buy but I wish for so much less and in other ways so much more.

Had David loved me? Hadn't we both fallen madly in love with one another? Hadn't we both felt the heedless passions of youth overtake our senses? Isn't that what brings people together at the beginning? Passion – that age-old charlatan that leaves you strengthened in the bloom of love then wanes when that tender bloom cannot weather the unmerited gales of change. Loving David plunged me relentlessly toward greater passions and even greater sorrows for which I was unprepared. Perhaps, neither was he. Oh, David I cannot consider these thoughts right now. *Expectation is the root of all heartache...* My own expectations, I was bored with life to the point where I was willing to confer my lifestyle unto a husband that seemed eager to receive it and still appreciated me for who I was. I expected him to continue to do so no matter what. *Some rise by sin, and some by virtue fall...* I did love him, and I know he did love me, but life changed everything, and our marriage lacked the ingredients to sustain the changes. Things like intimacy and trust, understanding, and the ability to communicate were never developed between us. We didn't really talk and neither did we take the time to listen. We failed to offer up our entire selves to this marriage. It is unfortunate, but it is too late now; I want to imagine that that part of my life never happened. He needs to let go and imagine the same thing. I just wish to be left in peace. I miss his love but peace does not seem to result from its absence.

From the balcony this morning I watch the sun rising slowly to the east where the fog is still sleeping in the leafless woods giving the air a soft, peach glow. I half expect this radiant blush to provide some warmth but early spring is still too timid to accept the sun's hearty embrace. Pulling my shawl more tightly around my shoulders I return to the music room to pick up this morning's paper and continue to read it inside where it is warm.

"Camellia Sylvester-Timmons, Furniture Heiress in Bed with Politics," was this morning's society column headline. Dear Camellia, my childhood friend, what has happened? We've drifted so far apart. As children we lived in one another's dreams. If one week she fantasized about being a princess, then we would break into our mothers' jewelry and adorn ourselves with baubles of every size, shape and color. We would practice dancing at a ball in front of large mirrors and then we would order servants to fan us while we took our tea. If the next week I fancied the idea of traveling on an African safari we would assemble all of our toy wildlife in the back gardens and using an old pram we would take turns ushering each other through the perilous landscape. Back then we were closer than sisters, especially closer than the sister with whom I shared a womb. I told Camellia secrets I wouldn't dream of telling anyone else.

Camellia's life took a different turn than my own. Her marriage to Walter Timmons seemed like the perfect match. They were compatible in every respect. He held the same broadminded principles as she did, even if their shared principles were self-contradicting. She would participate in marches against empirical and elitist oppression and Walter would support her ideals while their own servants, it was said, were among the lowest paid and most ill-used in London. Now, it seems, according to this article, she has joined the Women's Social and Political Union; she has become a suffragette and is charming several members of Parliament by financially supporting their socialist causes. If I know my old friend Camellia, it is more important to her to participate in the trendy circles of the moment than to consider this cause as a worthy human rights issue. For Camellia, socialist ideals provide one with the opportunity to continue living as one pleases and at the same time feel good about oneself because at least something is being done about the problems.

Since relinquishing my old circles, my friendships, my marriage, my lifestyle, my own ideals and my dreams, I must admit that my present circle is poor indeed but my spirit remains burdened. If I had the courage I would throw off what remains of this way of life and find a way to live in a circle of hope, the kind that grows larger through poverty of spirit. If life then wishes to inhabit my unoccupied soul, it had better give me a good reason.

# 23

## *Old Befana*

For many of us the child we once were forever lives inside our hearts. It is that child who laughs when something bizarre happens, who silently weeps when there is an injustice, who rejoices when dreams are realized, and certainly it is the child within us that mourns for each of our losses. Of course, there are those whose greatest loss is the child within and I believe they suffer the most. It becomes very difficult for those bereft of the inner child to withstand the untrustworthiness of life. Children carry with them anticipation like it is a part of their skin – it is the glow of promise and hope.

This child, Nolly, has a secret she is not sharing, not even with me. The secret lives inside her imagination, it shapes the way she thinks and feels and it holds together the pieces that assemble her courage. Each day she looks a little brighter than the day before; she takes on new challenges and makes the world the place where she wants to live happily.

Today, given a soft cloth for shining she sings her way up the stairs of the family quarters (where she's been told it is not necessary for her to be). Ivy is at the market just down the road and Nolly takes this opportunity to discover where her imagination will lead her, for imaginations can only stretch more comfortably when no one is directing them. She is no longer an orphaned child living in a stately manor because of someone's charity. For the moment there is no part of her that recalls the hardship during the few short years of her life. At this moment she is an unnamed fuzzy creature that crawls on all fours rather than walks, who looks carefully behind her should any fuzzy-creature-eating predator be following her for teatime purposes. She knows that she must be careful of the dust bunnies that her auntie has warned her about for they grow and grow and they eat anything that is left lying about so that you can never find your belongings again. Suddenly she is at the top of a hill (the stairs) and looking down she makes certain that her tail is intact for she felt something tugging at it on the way up.

The woods of this old attic are quite dark but from the dim light coming through a small octagonal window on the other side of the room, the fuzzy creature can see that there are giants in here (a stack of crates that must contain some other fuzzy creatures), a strange looking catapult like she'd seen outside the ruins of a castle (really it's an old pram mounded on top of some dusty furniture) and of all things bizarre and wonderful – a miniature replica of the train that rode past her old house where she and her Mommy worked to get food. The child is suddenly delighted and transformed from fuzzy creature to Alice in a world of magic. She is suddenly captivated by things she has only seen in shop windows and only dreamt of touching. The child approaches the train set slowly as if she expects that her presence will make it disappear, for surely its realism can only be dependent on her absence. She must be very quiet, for she knows she does not belong here. There is a chest in which she sees a set of carved wooden animals, a broken top, an old tea set wrapped in paper, and worn out wooden blocks with letters on them. Then, with the very tip of her finger she touches the mane of a wooden rocking horse until her eyes land on a treasure the very sight of which she will cherish forever. Suddenly, her hands cup her cheeks in amazement. It is that moment when you see with your eyes open what you've only imagined with your eyes closed; it is an instant of true astonishment in any child's life. Though I've yet to witness this child as speechless, I can see that her mind is racing with make-believe possibilities that words cannot keep pace with. She must not touch it; she can only drink it in with her eyes which have now become glossy for she's quite forgotten to blink. It is... of all things... a house! It looks much like the one she is now living in but it is smaller than herself (not by much!) and it is painted in the most delightful rose color which even in this gloomy attic she can see. "Haaaaa," she exhales. "It can't be real. It is too wonderful."

She begins to wonder if there are small families that live in this little house, a home where dreams are safe, where daddies stay put and mommies hold you close until you're ready to go, where babies crawl about and play at living a carefree life or cry because they think they need something. Perhaps there are little animals nibbling at sacks of grain in the cellars; maybe there's a granddad snoring in a worn out chair near the stove or a young man reading adventure stories by a dim lamp. Somewhere in the house the mommy and daddy kiss each other because it's the kisses that hold their little world together. She imagines a lifetime of toing and froing in the blink of a child's eye.

"Nolly!" Suddenly her auntie is summoning her back to the big house where very few people live. "Nolly, where are you?"

Once again she becomes a mysterious fuzzy creature retreating from the world of a cherished child. She crawls backward out of the attic and down the stairs, still in a state of dreaminess and wonder. She can hear Ivy calling her from the other side of the house but she cannot reply. She hasn't turned back into Nolly yet and she's reluctant to do so. Slowly, she crawls backwards down the carpeted hallway through the archway which leads into the servants' quarters. There are tall figures which fortify this hallway, a suit of armor from medieval times, statues of partially clad ladies hewn from ivory, and a massive mahogany clock at the center of the hallway which towers over the grand staircase. The child nearly bumps into the tall pedestal that supports a vase filled with ceramic Capodimonte flowers from Naples. Thankfully, she averts a disaster which could hurt her and her chances for remaining in this house.

Just as she passes through the archway separating the guest wing from the grand corridor, Ivy is at her side. "Where have you been, my sweet?"

The child looks up innocently as most children do when they've been exploring. "I'm a fuzzy creature capturing the dust bunnies," she says, and she holds up her soft cloth (which was still clean).

Ivy takes the child by the hand. "Come. I've brought you something special from the market. It's a bit of maple caramel. It was my favorite when I first came to England."

"Do you still like them?" Nolly asks.

"I do. But, I was just a young girl when I came here and I thought they were the grandest thing I'd ever tasted."

"Have you tasted something grander?"

"Lately, I've quite forgotten what grand tastes like. I want to see if you think they're grand!"

# 24

## *Ivy*

Nolly is an intuitive and clever child. Her questions are relentless and quite perceptive. Why did your mistress go away? Why is this house so big if no one else lives here? If she lives alone why does she need a servant? Are there no other children in this house? Why not? Who are the three little girls in the painting in the hall? Why do two of them look exactly alike? Where did they go? How did the big horse get into the front hall? Was he once a real horse? Where does your mistress go for so long? Does she play the piano in the other room? Can I play it?

When she's not asking never-ending questions she is inventing a succession of stories and when she tells them I don't think she takes a single breath in between; at other times she is singing happily for the sheer sake of singing. Considering the harshness of the life she's had and the fact that her mother has only recently passed she seems such a pleasant child. She speaks often of Colleen, sometimes as if she is still nearby, and retells the stories her mother had told her. It is very difficult to distinguish between the stories of pure imagination and those that are real. At times there is a frivolous blend of both – like the story about the man that God loved and the man put all the animals in a boat except for snakes. Snakes are bad, she says. After God made the flood the snakes learned to swim and they all swam to Ireland and they stayed there until St. Paddy chased them out.

I give my sister credit for blessing her daughter with the softness of make-believe so that she would not notice the sharp edges of misfortune until it became necessary. It wasn't that way with us back home in Wicklow. There was no opportunity for turning our faces away from the daily slog of life. In my heart I do believe that my brothers, Tim and Aidan, set off with Danny to fight in the north so that they could help reclaim the joy that comes from freedom and escape the bleakness of futility. Pa would often tell them, "Every man has a right to the dignity Almighty God gave him. There is no dignity in coercion and domination that the State imposes." Ma would tell him to hush. "Liam, they're just young lads. They don't need to know such things until they're older." But Pa would insist that when they grew older it would be too late, too late to do a good thing, he'd say. They'd be in the habit of unconcern by then. I suspect that my mother understood the need to encourage them to stand for something but she also understood the value of preserving youth for once it grows away from us it never returns.

At fourteen, I'd finished primary school. Though I was told I was quite clever, I wasn't interested in continuing, I'd had enough. I was never one to daydream about marriage, finding the right boy and settling down with as many children as God should give us, and struggling daily to figure out how to feed them. I figured I could work to supply the needs of one mouth easily enough and going into service was my escape. When I saw the ad in the post office that the Barrington's had placed, I responded, and before my parents could raise a word of objection I was on a boat for England. I've never regretted my decision; the Barrington family when they were here were all so good to me; the other servants left me be to do my own work in housekeeping and I've never gone a day without food or a soft bed to lie down upon.

Because I wasn't the oldest in my family, I'd escaped the steady wheel of expectations. After what happened to my older brother, Killian, I rather disappeared from my parents' view. Once they'd been forced to face the horror of it all, they began to focus steadily on Tim and Aidan. Things were never the same. Pa tried to forget Killian and kept trying to help his other boys move forward, move away from Wicklow, find their lives. Pa had begun languishing though I didn't know why at the time. Ma wore a face frozen in grief as if time had stopped at that moment she'd learned that Killian was gone. She continued the routines of life; she spoke and fed us, cleaned, washed and ironed, but what made her Ma was no longer there. She tried to keep Colleen a child for as long as she could. Growing up meant loss.

I'd seen Killian only once that morning as he was coming back from the fields. He loved the earth and everything about it. He loved working the land and caring for the animals; life revolved around the rising of the sun and its setting, the glow of the moon and the stars. Rain, wind, and clouds were his companions, and to make all of these loves richer he'd added Taira, the seventeen year-old love of his life. She was a beauty; her hair was thick and lush, the color of rich soil and she had deep eyes to match. Her skin was pale and delicate like the softest satin and her smile could bring down the arrogance of a rainbow. She was perfect as far as Killian was concerned. All he wanted in the world was to marry Taira and live off the land. I do believe that Taira loved Killian, too, or he would have seen through any deceit. He knew things for what they were; he understood what was at the root of something in front of him just by looking at it. Love was not the issue – it was a conflict of dreams. He wanted home, family and the land, and she wanted to partake in an idea placed into her mind by Alistair McShane which involved going to America. Alistair was funny, adventurous, and charming. He offered her marriage and excitement. Killian was warm, loving, and as steady as an oak but one whose roots reached deep into the bedrock of Ireland. She chose Alistair, though she did not love him. It was that aspect of the rejection from which Killian could not recover – that she would choose *anything else* over the love they shared. After she'd left he found no more joy in the earth, no more splendor in the seasons, and no more reason to continue life. When Killian didn't come in for supper, Pa went out to the barn and found my dear older brother swinging from a rope tied to the beams. I will never forget the cry that came from Pa's soul. He'd lost his firstborn, the one to take over the bit of land. Everything he'd worked hard to build for so many years didn't matter anymore. Nothing mattered after that day. Killian took Pa's charted future with him, and it didn't make a difference what any of us did after that; it wasn't part of Pa's plan. From that time on our family was broken because one member had severed the thread of hope that held us together. At fourteen, I left home. And through the years I've seen what's happened to the Barringtons. Much the same, really. My mistress and I grapple along, side by side, with a sense of resignation to the variables in life and we try to stay within the structured haven as much as we can, that is, until this darling little girl came to this house.

These circumstances, with Nolly here, are causing me some concern. Though the child entertains herself quite well, I fear she must be lonely. I don't have the time to sit with her and play as she'd like, and often my duties take me away from her for short periods of time. She is left to her own imagination most of the day while I work to keep up with the housework and corresponding with my mistress and running to the post to forward her important mail; this leaves the little one in this enormous house to wander about. Nolly no longer has her mother to care for her, nor are there children nearby with whom she can play. She drifts through the house with that "granny" statue in her hand or pocket and carefully designs an intricate world of make-believe.

While I know she would invent a story if I asked her directly, I suspect that she's been to the family quarters of the house, and possibly sneaked up into the attic where many remnants lie in storage and I know my mistress would probably have us both out of the house if she knew her personal space was being invaded. I must have a stern talk with Nolly about respecting the privacy of others, especially before my mistress returns in a month's time. Nolly has made this her own private patch and I deplore the idea of limiting her access. It is becoming quite clear that I cannot offer this child what she really needs; I am an inadequate auntie and a house alone cannot take the place of what a small child really needs. Nolly needs a sense of belonging. I can tell her about our family in Wicklow but all in the past tense. So much of the story is best laid to rest. From what I've observed of this little child she seems to need a sense of belonging about her faith as well. Colleen planted some very fine seeds about trusting God but what am I to do? I've told myself for many years that it's enough just to be a good person. How can I share with Nolly that which I seem to have lost along the way, the very core of goodness? Where would I begin? Nolly loves the little nuggets of faith she has received so far and she has a right to learn how to be more than just a good person. I know we're meant to be more than that but I don't know how she will learn it here, in *this house* or from me.

## 25

## *Margaret*

A temporary arrangement has been made for me to visit Camellia's Aunt Bess who now resides in a home for the aged. Honestly, with all that family money, couldn't a little of it be spent on a nursing staff to care for this poor old woman in her own home? I have not spoken with Camellia directly; I have no wish to do so, but I have had brief contact with Gentleman Sam her older brother who is confined to a wheelchair because of a childhood illness. For as long as I can remember everyone called him "Gentleman Sam" instead of his given name Jonas and the reasons have varied. For one, he wished to be distinguished from his father, Jonas, so he went by his middle name, Samuel. Secondly, he always smiled and bowed his head formally whenever spoken to so as to validate a person's salutations, statements, or departures. He himself is not much of a conversationalist but he is a gentleman to a fault when it comes to others' ramblings; he listens, smiles, and nods.

As I have no desire to be unnecessarily sociable, I simply want to fill some part of my days with a modicum of goodwill; I've sent a note to Gentleman Sam and asked if I could gain access as an authorized visitor at the private nursing home to visit with his Aunt Bess, and he agreed. His response simply read *Yes, I will advise the nursing staff of your forthcoming visits. Sincerely, Samuel.* If one did not know of his genteel spirit, one would find his correspondence to be curt.

He is as different from Camellia as a rabbit from a chattering monkey. These days I don't genuinely miss my friendship with Camellia nor do I ever entertain the idea of reestablishing communication with her but I retain some deep nostalgic sentiments for her Aunt Bess, who, during my childhood, provided me with an abundance of memories to accompany me into adulthood. Aunt Bess was an artist who painted beautiful memories in other people's minds.

Though it was unbecoming of a lady of her social standing to devote her time to kitchen duties best left to a competent staff, Aunt Bess loved to spend endless hours learning to cook exotic foods. Her husband, Uncle George, was a foreign dignitary and for many years they had traveled around the globe. Aunt Bess brought each experience home in the form of a new culinary adventure. If she visited India she would saturate the house with the smell of curry, cardamom, cloves, cinnamon, mint, ginger and other mysterious spices. Her first attempt was an entrée of Chicken Balti preceded by Tarka Dal and accompanied by Sweet Lassi. The flavors of such dishes were an excursion for the palate. Her simulation of the experience did not end with merely preparing unknown repasts; she would recreate the very environment inside her home to look like India. Bolts of brightly-colored silks would be draped along the walls in a scalloped fashion. The lush plants of Bangalore such as Java Plum Tree; ferns, palms, and hibiscus plants would be interspersed among statues of Shiva, Nataraja, and Kamalasana Chaturbhuja Ganesha. Aunt Bess would dress in a Nivi style Sari of either a bold violet or red or a combination of the two. Best of all, she returned with a hired musician to play Sarangi music during the banquet. Stepping into Aunt Bess's home was like stepping into another world, a changing world, and each experience was in itself life-changing. On one of her trips to India, she'd visited the tomb of St. Thomas at Santhome – the very apostle of Christ who had exclaimed "My Lord and my God" after doubting the news that Jesus had risen. She had been moved very deeply by her visit to that site, she'd said. She told us quite seriously that St. Thomas had trusted because of what he'd seen but we can trust in the truth because of its fruits. Though it may be hard to *see* these fruits we can feel them growing inside us. At the time I had no idea what she was talking about but I did know that I felt something growing inside me when I was around her. She spoke of her experiences with such animated expressions and then suddenly she would grow somber. In her mind she was reliving the actual moment of seeing St. Thomas' tomb and you could feel her plummet from the heights of fascination to the depths of solemn reverence. Aunt Bess had a talent for bringing the actual sensations into the moment. I always felt like I had *been there*. The Indian festivities would go on for months until either Aunt Bess tired of "staying" in the same place, or it was time to actually travel with Uncle George to another land once again.

One of my favorite memories of a dinner party at Aunt Bess's home was upon her return from Greece. She'd visited Crete and Mykonos and Santorini (the city on the hill) and Rhodes, among other famous places. The sari was packed away, the silk drapes came down, the plants were donated to the botanical gardens and the curry smell was almost forgotten when she ordered all accessories to be donated to local charities, especially homes for children and the elderly. She then hired some local builders to install Corinthian style pillars in the sitting room and dining room, tear down the wallpaper and paint the rooms the color blue the likes of which I'd never seen. Oh, she worked night and day with the painters to get just the right blue – the one from Santorini that was so deep and rich you could almost taste it. The wooden and carpeted floors were ripped out and sent to warm the floors of a women's shelter and stone floors were installed. Uncle George was so overwhelmed with her latest transformation that he moved into a small apartment until *this passed*. It may have seemed like extravagance, but to Aunt Bess it was her way of giving all she could; it was a gift. This was an integral part of who she was and she wanted to share this part of herself without restraint. She was generous beyond measure. What made these feasts so special wasn't just the food, (in this case, the extraordinary olives, cheese, and wine that she brought back) it was the guests. She did not have a wide circle of elitist friends adept at formalities and party performances. Aunt Bess shared these experiences with simple friends that stopped by to say hello, the servants, the occasional tourist that happened to be walking by her house, but also the people who happened to be sitting in the doorways of the local churches waiting for some food. She invited *people* into her home, not official guests. Her magic was in her ability to create a culture in her home and everyone was welcome. Each person would walk away more cultivated and lifted to new heights. She was enchanting!

At the Wellworth Home for the Aged I was unprepared for the sight of her new surroundings. This exceptional woman who had enriched my youth with wonder was relegated to a small crowded room comprised of meager necessities. When I walked into her room, I must have gasped for several vacant eyes looked up in my direction. Which of these was Aunt Bess? These surroundings were an indignity to the soul of any human, let alone Aunt Bess.

# 26

## *Ivy*

Nolly and I had our first test-of-wills today. I'd gone to the bank to pay a few small debts for my mistress. While walking down Walnut St. to Adams I was abruptly confronted by a peddler pushing his cart full of woolen shawls. "Winter's a'comin' lass," he said, "it's not too soon to buy your wares. Don't wait till it's too late – the price will go up. Get a shawl now for 4 shillings." I tried to get past him without looking at his eyes, for then they could reel you in, and I did not speak a yay or nay, I tried to hurry along to sidestep him altogether. But then there were two of them, one in front of me and one to the side and they would not let me pass. I should have taken the long route to the bank, I've encountered such hooligans before but I did not want to take any longer than necessary, leaving Nolly alone at home.

Finally, I spoke up as loudly as possible so that others might hear. "Let me pass. I do not want your shawls. Leave me be!" Furiously, I wriggled away by stepping back and running past the one to my side. Awful men. I ran briskly down Adams St. not wishing to be detained a moment longer when a deluge of rain hit just before I stepped into the bank. Thankfully, the bank was not crowded and Mr. Trumble was available at his window. He was experienced with the normal business dealings I must manage for Mrs. Livingston and the estate. I was flushed when I stepped up to the counter.

"Is everything all right, Miss O'Neill? You seem out of breath. Please, take your time. There is no line, today."

"Thank you, Mr. Trumble. I'm fine now. It has started to rain heavily. Thank you for your patience." I looked in my bag for the pouch that held the money Mrs. Livingston had left for me to pay the gaslight bill. The pouch was not in my bag. Swiftly, I turned around to see if I'd dropped it on the floor behind me as I entered the bank but saw nothing. I looked in my bag again, rummaging around as if the smaller items could somehow hide the large pouch. My breath stopped and a feeling of coldness spread into my chest and limbs. For a moment, I could not speak.

"Miss O'Neill? Might you have forgotten the funds?"

"No, Mr. Trumble. I've forgotten nothing. Pardon me a moment." There were two people standing behind me now, rather drenched from the rain. I let them pass ahead of me while I strode stiffly toward the door. I opened the door to the bank and stepped out into the rain. There was no pouch on the street. I walked down a ways as if in a daze and turned onto Adams. The woolen scarf peddlers were nowhere in sight. Few people were on the street now that the rain had hit with such ferocity. I walked down to the stationhouse in front of which I had been accosted by the two peddlers. No pouch, no peddlers, no funds to pay my mistress's bills. I gulped down the scream I wanted to shout out and it felt as if it scratched my throat. What would I tell Mrs. Livingston? I didn't have additional funds to pay the bills in the event of an emergency. Her creditors were few, but they needed paying on time. I stood in the middle of Adams St. in the pouring down rain and felt the weight of something much heavier than just my present predicament. It is at times such as these that what has passed now assaults us with greater force; all my struggles to better my life have led me to the point where I'm standing in the middle of Adams St. with a botched routine duty. Mrs. Livingston is kind but I fear her present state of mind is in no condition to tolerate incompetence. I had no idea how to proceed: go back to the bank and reveal my shame to Mr. Trumble and implore his advice, or go back home and face whatever consequences may befall me when Mrs. Livingston returns in a few short weeks? What was old Mr. Trumble to say? I have no authority to transfer funds out of Mrs. Livingston's account to cover the charges. Well, at least he deserved an explanation for my sudden departure and for Mrs. Livingston's bills going into arrears. With head down I walked once again toward the bank. I was soaked through the inner tissues of my skin by the time I arrived and it seemed that Mr. Trumble could read my woes upon my face.

"Miss O'Neill, may I get you a cup of tea?"

"I beg your pardon, Mr. Trumble, as much as I would love a cup of tea, I'm afraid I must return home to sort out my difficulties. I was... intercepted... by two men... on my way to the bank and it seems that the funds I carried were ..." I was trying to look for the right word. Stolen, seized, pilfered, misappropriated?

"I see," replied Mr. Trumble. Yes, he had the look of an older man who condescends upon a child who should have known to be more careful.

I held up my head now and looked directly into his eyes. "I will sort this out and return as soon as I am able, Mr. Trumble. Good day."

His scorn might have been the result of my imagination acting upon my own embarrassment. He was as powerless as I am. I felt dishonored and abused. And now my thoughts turned to Nolly. I've been trying the best I can to manage the house and all of my mistress's affairs in her absence. Normally, it is plenty enough but now I must think of the little one. She needs so much more than I can offer and she certainly should not be left alone or to her own little schemes while I clean and run errands. I picked up my pace and hurried into the house. I needed to change into a different set of garments before I should catch a chill.

"Nolly? My darling, where are you?" She is never in the same place I've left her; I knew well enough to expect that. "Nolly?" I left her with a list of things to be done in my absence. Oh, I don't really expect a small child to work – that would be cruel. But, she likes to think she is helping me and it gives me some comfort knowing that she will gradually learn responsibility. "Nolly, where are you?" I could see from the kitchen that she'd begun tackling the list I'd told her to tend to. The peelings from last night's potatoes and the bone from the stew were taken out to the bin near the kitchen door. She'd put her bowl from breakfast into the basin. And it looked like she'd taken her favorite rose-colored soft cloth for her morning "shining" which usually turned into an umbrella on her imaginary rainy days, or a blanket for granny if her "old bones were feeling cold," or most often it becomes a satchel full of trifles she finds around the house to give as gifts. "Nolly?" I couldn't hear her singing or chattering or playing in the service area of the home. She was nowhere to be found in the washroom or the cupboards or storage areas. I looked in the front part of the house – she was not in the study or the parlor, nor had she built a secret castle from the dining hall chairs today. The antechamber showed signs of her having been present for the candlesticks and photographs on the side table had been rearranged again even though I'd expressly told her not to touch these things that do not belong to us. There was a book from the study which had been left on the chair. It was her favorite book from the lower shelves within her reach: *Tess of the D'Urbervilles*. Though it will be many years before she can read this book, I've been told it is her favorite because of the book jacket. It has a brick colored covering dotted with little black shamrocks, a lion with a long tail standing on its hind legs in the crest, and a flowing ribbon with the girl's name on it. I'd told Nolly that the girl in this book had the name of Tess and Nolly said, "That is such a sensible name." Where do small children come up with such responses? *"Nolly?"*

A sense of panic had now begun to affect my breathing with swift, sharp breaths and my head was still spinning from my trip to the bank. From the front hall I climbed the stairs to the main corridor. The last time I'd left her alone she'd been crawling away from the family quarters and I'd eventually reminded her not to visit that part of the house. She'd promised me she would keep out of *people's privacy*. I turned into the guest wing and searched through each room – she was nowhere. "Nolly? Tell auntie where you are. I cannot find you, little one. I promise I won't be annoyed if you tell me where you are. *Now!*" I could not seem to help the impatience creeping into my voice. I really did not have time for searching games; I still had so much to do in addition to finding a resolution to this morning's money problem. I headed for the family wing and called out but there was no response. When she does hear me, she does respond so it was becoming quite clear that she was not in the house. She knows, she *knows* she is not to go outside at all when I am not at home. Besides, it is raining. Merciful God, please let me find her well. "Nolly!"

I ran down to the kitchen to look out of the back door. "Nolly!" I continued shouting. Suddenly a small voice rang from the greenhouse at the other end of the garden. "Auntie, here I am." I finally exhaled a wad of relief. I grabbed an umbrella from the stand near the door and ran through the muddy, neglected garden to the greenhouse.

"Nolly, my love, what are you doing out here?" I did not even give her a chance to answer. I grabbed her by the hand and pulled her back to the house with me. Once inside the kitchen I examined her. She was fine, dry, and unharmed, but I was angry and she began to pull a melancholy face.

"I told you to never go outside the house when I am gone."

"You told me you'd never be gone long," she retorted. Where on earth had she learned how to give me cheek? She'd never done so before. Now, recalling the reasons for my delay I was even more upset – with her, with myself, with the thieves, with Mr. Trumble, with my mistress, and with anyone who came into my thoughts. And Nolly bore the brunt of it.

"You do not speak to me in such a way, Nolly. Remember that! I gave you very strict rules to follow: places in the house and the outdoors are restricted to you when I'm not at home, the mistress's special things that must not be touched or moved, books that must not leave the study... Shall I go on? You have been disobeying all the rules and now I find you in the greenhouse. You are never to go in there, Nolly. Do you understand? There may be things that are harmful to children, poisons, gardening tools, *and rubbish* for heaven's sake. Are you listening to me?"

The child stood very quiet during my diatribe. She did not flinch or cry. She simply stood there staring into my eyes with a saddened calmness. "I asked you a question, Nolly. Are you listening to me?"

She nodded her head slowly and remained standing in front of me without a word. What is one supposed to do after one scolds a child, I wondered? I do not believe I am cut out for this. Was I supposed to resume casual conversation or engage in deliberate silence? It seemed that second-guessing my own actions was the natural course of action that followed. Had I been too harsh? Was she right that I had promised I'd never leave her for long and that I was the first to break the promise? Was she too young to remember rules for a longer length of time? Suddenly, I felt remorseful. It wasn't the child's fault; it was entirely my own. I reached out to touch her arm and draw her near but she backed away and went into the room we shared, sat on her cot, and wept silently.

I stood up slowly and brushed my apron. I had twenty duties to attend to today and I'd failed to complete any of them thus far. This was not going to be a productive day, I decided. I walked into our small bedchamber. Nolly was sniffling quietly. I sat on my bed across from her cot.

"Nolly," I began. I did not know where to go from that point on. The truth might be a good place to begin. "I'm sorry I was cross. I was very upset because I did not know where to find you and I became very frightened. I was also upset because the rules I put in place are meant to keep you safe from harm and I don't want anything to happen to you. If something should happen to you I would be very, very sad. I am no longer angry. I was just very scared. Do you understand?"

Finally, she looked up at me with large tears trickling heavily down her cheeks.

"You needn't cry anymore. I'm no longer angry."

"I'm not crying about that," she said.

"Then why are you crying?" I asked. She knitted her eyebrows and looked at me harshly.

"Granny is still out in the greenhouse."

# 27

## Old Befana

I've been left lying about in many strange places, but an old, cracked chamber pot is a first. I don't even want to think about what passed this way before me. This place is damp and unkempt with a definite smell of decay coming from somewhere. It's no place for a child but her intentions were good. Everything in the big house is clean and shiny and posh. It was this old glass house in disrepair that needed a "bit of shining" as she put it. Children can get into such bad trouble, not because of their own bad intentions, but because of the oversights of others.

Not long ago, I found myself in the company of a young black girl from the Sudan. This child had a smile that could light up a moonless night. She was dearly loved by her family and they rarely let her out of their sight but those were dangerous times for young black children. This child had such a deep inner calm that she flitted through life as if she were already living in heaven. She had no eyes for danger, could not recognize mischief, and she certainly had no suspicious bones in her tiny body. She was a bubble of fluttering joy. The greatest quality of this sweet child was her helpful and obliging spirit. If anyone was feeling sad, she would cheer them with her smile. If someone was sick she would help them, bring them tea and do anything she could to comfort them; if someone asked for a favor she would be the first to volunteer.

It was a combination of her trusting spirit and her eagerness to help that put this little one into jeopardy one day. While out near the river fetching water for a tired old man in her village she encountered several strange men on camels who asked her kindly if she could get them some water, too. She smiled at them and went back to the river for more water. When she brought her vessel with fresh, cool water to the men, they seized her, bound her, and took her to their camp and later sold her into slavery. By the time I encountered this sweet, little child – oh, the things she had endured. I could see from her many scars – bad scars – that she had been wounded deeply. But the little one still smiled, still carried the goodness of an innocent child that openly shares the beauty within her. She'd been bought and sold by Arab merchants time and again and forced to give homage to a god she did not comprehend. After being sold off to various cruel masters, she finally ended up in the service of a kind man; he was some type of important person from Italy and he would soon return there. After he bought her he gave her as a gift to a friend of his and the sweet little thing took up residence in Italy for a while. It was there that I came to know her. Not a day went by that I didn't witness the core gentleness of this little girl. Even after all she'd been through she still had an infectious smile and she went out of her way to help others. It was as if she had this secret, this inner knowledge that no matter what happened she would be all right in the end. Within this new home, she'd learned about that caring God and it was her smile that showed me how secure she felt in his love. Somehow she'd always known that he was there, that no matter what happened to her person, there was something inside her being that belonged to him and she wanted to belong to him completely! She didn't know it but it was also something I needed to feel at the time. Her name was Bhakita and it seemed that God had created this little girl to be all heart.

One day while on an errand for her mistress, this darling girl witnessed a sight worse than the scars on her small body – she witnessed poverty, hunger and disease. Even though she now lived in the comfort of a caring home she saw in the streets of her new village that there were children who had no homes, no clothing and no food. They'd been abandoned to the streets like discarded rubbish with no purpose. At a nearby convent there were a group of sisters that reminded me of those old spinsters back in my hometown. They came along lifted these children from the gutters with such tenderness as if they were picking delicate flowers from a garden and carried them to shelter and safety. Bhakita's heart wrenched for these little children and she yearned to be like the sisters. Then and there this child vowed that if she ever had the opportunity to join these sisters and help the poor in some way she would do it! I wanted to spend more time with her, to learn from her, but I ended up in a box at a jumble sale not long after I met her.

## 28

## *Margaret*

A clock is ticking loudly in the hall just outside Aunt Bess's room. I now see that Aunt Bess is sitting by a window wrapped in a brown woolen coverlet even though the late summer warmth is still embracing the air. There are five beds in this small room and each one is filled except for the one near the steel metal cabinet. I walk quietly through a sparsely furnished room and pass by the bedridden ladies, three of them are staring at me and one is turned on her side looking into a pervasive void. It is difficult in this muted room to see the color of the walls or the floor. There is very little which suggests life in this unlit chamber except for the afternoon glow which shines on a tree outside the small window where Aunt Bess is sitting. She turns her head in my direction and squints her eyes into the dim light of the room. She does not immediately recognize me for it has been many years, but I also wonder whether she is capable of remembering me at all or if age has tampered with her mind.

"Aunt Bess?" I call her by the only title I've ever known. She wasn't my own aunt but everyone called her Aunt Bess. That designation would not be helpful to her in trying to figure out who might be addressing her. Within moments a cheery smile stretches across her face and she puts her hands up to her head!

"Margaret!" She then covers her mouth with her hands while she laughs. "Oh, dear Margaret, is that really you?" I can't believe she not only recognizes me after all this time, but remembers my name.

"Aunt Bess," I say, barely above a whisper. My heart is thumping. I can't seem to get any more words out, choked as I am with emotion.

"Pull a chair over here and sit for a while, my dear. What a tremendous surprise! I am so delighted to see you, child. Come sit closer, we don't want to disturb the party girls!" She nods her head toward her roommates and lets out another laugh.

"Aunt Bess," I repeat. There were a million thoughts going through my mind but I cannot voice any of them. Fortunately, I don't need to speak; she seems so willing to talk as if she hasn't been able to do so in ages, there are streams of information beginning to spill out.

"Uncle George passed away three years ago. It will be three years in November. He was very sick, my dear. He had throat cancer and then it spread to other parts of his body, his lungs, and oh, my poor George, he suffered so. He was too dignified to complain, though, Margaret. He was terribly sick. Never one utterance of complaint. He'd simply smile at me when I sat beside him and he'd squeeze my hand when it was time for me to let him sleep. I miss him so much. He was my world. You know we met when I was just sixteen. He was already in his Majesty's service by then and one day when he came home to Ulverston he said, Bessy, let's get married. And so we did, right then and there, we were married. Oh, my mother had such an awful time of it, you know. I was meant to get married in the church you see but there was no time. George was serving under Lord Raglan at the time in the Crimean War and he did not have sufficient leave for a proper wedding and honeymoon, so we ran down to the magistrate and asked him to officiate. Back then, put a five pound note in anyone's pocket and they would marry you. But when he came home we did go to the church and received the sacrament – it is important, you know!" Aunt Bess smiles fondly now. "I miss my George so much now. We were married for sixty years you know. Oh, I do wish we'd been blessed with children but it was never meant to be." She stops suddenly and looks at me and takes my hands into her own. "How are you my dear?"

"Fine, Aunt Bess. I was spending some time at the summer home in Grange and I thought I'd pop over here to see you, to see how you're doing. Gentleman Sam told me where to find you."

"Ah, yes, my loquacious nephew," she says sarcastically which makes me laugh unexpectedly. "How is he? And how is my niece, Camellia? I hope they are doing well. I never hear from them, nor do they visit. Well, with Sam I can understand, it is difficult for him to get around but Camellia… Though, she was never very dependable when it came to family, especially aging aunties. I'm sorry, dear, I know she was your dearest friend. I shouldn't talk like this. I'd heard about your…"

"Aunt Bess, I've come to visit *you*," I interrupt her quickly. "I wanted to see how you are doing – I'm ashamed it's been too long. How are you? Are they caring for you well here?"

"I'm perfectly fine, my dear. There isn't a stitch out of place. I have my faculties," pointing to her head, "and my health couldn't be better." I sit quietly waiting for her to continue.

"You're probably wondering what I'm doing in a place like this." She sighs and looks out the window again. "I suppose I was a very foolish lady, wasn't I? Without children to care for me, there is no one to turn to at this stage of my life. I am here because of the generosity of my nephew and niece. They pay a fee to the folks that run this place, to take care of me. I had nowhere else to go. There was nothing left at the end when George died. Nothing. I'd spent money all along and I had to sell the house, do you remember my house on Brickman

Street, dear? I sold it off to cover medical expenses and funeral costs for my dear George."

"Surely you have something coming in from Uncle George's retirement? I'm sorry; it is none of my business, Aunt Bess. Forgive me."

She pats my hand firmly. "Nonsense. We're family, let's not have such talk." She reaches up and pinches my cheek. "I understand that whatever comes in each month from George's retirement is being used for my care in this facility and to settle any remaining debts. Gentleman Sam takes care of everything so that I don't have to worry about it."

I bite my lip to keep from stating the obvious. Gentleman Sam lives alone in his mansion, surely he has room for his aging aunt and *her* money could be spent on a private nurse, if needed. I feel inwardly outraged but I don't want to discolor my visit with Aunt Bess. Sensing my thoughts, Aunt Bess pinches my cheek again.

"Do you know where I got into to the habit of pinching cheeks," she asks brightly. She has not lost her vitality and exuberance in all these years. I smile. I believe I know the answer to her question.

"Remember when we came back from Italy?" She throws her head back and laughs. There are small tears leaking out of the corners of her laughing eyes. At the memory of her return from Italy I begin laughing, too. My heavens, I'm rather surprised that the muscles of my face still remember how to let bursts of humor escape from my chest. I put my free hand over my stomach for its unused muscles are suddenly in pain.

Aunt Bess continues reliving the memory. It was just a few short days after Christmas when she and Uncle George had returned from Umbria. Aunt Bess quickly set about tearing down the vestiges of her previous travels and started work on decorating for a new theme – Christmas in Italy. Camellia and I had heard the news of their return and quickly ran over to her lovely neo-classical house on Brickman St. We darted through the front gate and swept past the many shrubs and small trees that lined the front yard. Aunt Bess loved plants of any variety, whether they were accustomed to the climate of northwest England or not. There was very little grass or walking space – it was all filled with plants, shrubs and trees. Except for entrance on the north side of the house where very little could grow. This entrance was used for carrying in the souvenirs from her travels. Though, heaven help us, we never expected what she'd brought from Italy.

The entryway of the house was affectionately called the neutral territory. It was furnished simply and without bias to any particular country. It remained the antechamber to a world of surprises. It gave away no clues. Camellia and I wanted to help set up the next feast. We might have been eleven or twelve at the time and as giggly as five year-olds. We couldn't wait to see what the latest trend would entail. A few of the poorer town folk were paid handsomely to help her set up her house each time she returned. They awaited her homecoming as anxiously as we did, perhaps even more so. That day they were setting up several Christmas trees, a variety of which I'd never seen before. Aunt Bess had returned with potted umbrella pines and cypress trees! They reached the ceiling of the magnificent great room. The task at hand, of course, meant decorating all of the trees for Christmas. Tiny candles, blown-glass ornaments, tinsel, ribbons, jewels and baubles of every shape and color adorned the trees in the room.

Camellia had shouted, "Aunt Bess, are you out of your mind? It's not Christmas anymore. It was done five days ago!" To which Aunt Bess had replied, "Hush child, we only have a few days left to get ready. Christmas is certainly NOT finished! It has only just begun! Don't just stand there; get to work!" So Camellia and I jumped in and started decorating. What a time we had. In my own home the servants generally put up one Christmas tree in the front hall and it was always a ruckus until they figured out where to put the large bronze horse until after Christmas. The holiday itself was a very cagey affair, with mother trying to keep it solemn and religious and father wanting to entertain his many business associates. The result was a negligible event that simply disrupted all our routines. The only reason I happened to be at Grange rather than London that year was precisely because Aunt Bess was scheduled to return from Italy and Camellia invited me to spend the Christmas holidays with her in anticipation of her next bash.

Within a few short days, the decorating was finished and a life-size hollow stable had been built beneath the beautifully decorated Christmas trees. We had even been given a mountain of cotton to spread along the floor and pull apart into pieces to embellish the trees. It was meant to simulate snow, and all of it looked lovely, like an enchanted forest steeped in mystery.

On the day of the celebration, it was the sixth of January already, (who could ever forget?) all the guests were told to wear the simplest clothing we owned. Camellia and I had to borrow some dresses from Levinia, one of Camellia's servants. We'd never been asked to dress down several social strata before. Naturally, we were curious. Upon our arrival we were told to be seated on the floor along the perimeter of the room. All of the furniture had been removed, and although it was a few degrees below freezing, all of the windows in the great hall were open. It was biting cold in that room. Camellia and I kept our coats on and huddled together in anticipation. Then it began. From the side entrance of the house and through the back corridor came a small donkey carrying woman (the daughter of Aunt Bess's friend Lizzy. It was said that she and Lizzy were best friends from childhood and both shared the same name – Elizabeth. To distinguish them, one went by Bess and the other by Lizzy. The daughter's name was Lily.) Lily was clearly playing the part of Mary and she was holding an actual baby! It was the child of Katherine, the housemaid's little boy, and he was kicking up a fuss. Alongside the donkey, Lily and the baby, Willie the gardener who was playing Joseph walked closely next to the mother and child, worried that with one wrong move on the part of the donkey the child might fall. A couple of men whom I did not recognize came in dressed like shepherds and oh my word, they brought actual sheep – living, breathing sheep – into the room. Everyone took their place in the stable. Aunt Bess and her sister, Camellia's mother Louise, came out next dressed as angels and singing *Gloria, in excelsis deo* and stood on either side of the scene. Camellia and I sat on that freezing cold floor with our mouths hanging wide open.

A man with a violin began to play *O Come All Ye Faithful*, and then John Henry Hopkins' hymn, *We Three Kings*. One at a time, three kings came into the room dressed in lavish clothes. They were poor, retired fishermen from the village but today they stood out royally among the rest of us who were dressed simply. First came Caspar, the oldest man, hunched over and dressed in purple gossamer fabric and carrying a gold box; then came Melchior, barely a bit younger who was dressed in white satin trimmed in gold and carrying frankincense, and finally Balthazar, a dark-skinned man dressed in red silk carrying myrrh. Most of the time when Aunt Bess had one of her celebrations I laughed and laughed. On this occasion, I remember, I wanted to cry. It was like being present at the actual moment when Jesus had his own first celebration! I sat very still, speechless like everyone else in the room while Aunt Bess told us about the Italian tradition of celebrating with gifts on the Feast of the Epiphany – not Christmas, because they believed that no one should receive their gifts before the Christ child. She told us about how St. Francis, the poor man from Assisi, was the first one to reenact the Nativity using real people and animals just as she had done today. She looked right at Camellia when she said that it remains

Christmas until the birthday boy gets his presents – the party isn't over until he says it is! At that point, each of the three kings came over to the guests sitting on the floor and opened their boxes for us to grab something from inside. It wasn't really gold, frankincense and myrrh, but it was little boxes of Torrone, a customary Christmas confection in Italy. Aunt Bess then told all of us children sitting on the floor that gold represents truth, and that the Baby Jesus was himself *truth*. Frankincense represents obedience and how this little baby always showed us how to be obedient to our parents. Finally, she told us that myrrh represents love because that was why Jesus was born – because God loves us so much. We were never to forget that, she said. Her words stuck out of the Christmas scene like a solitary star in the darkest sky. We couldn't look away from her shining eyes. We were mesmerized.

Then, when each of us had received our little box of candy treat we burst into a heartwarming rendition of *Joy to the World*. At that point, the Baby Jesus was really screaming, the sheep relieved themselves in the stable and the guests were ushered into the dining room to enjoy a sumptuous repast of Italian delicacies. Aunt Bess is now smiling as she finishes retelling the memory. I am feeling like I want to sit here forever. I have no desire to end my modicum of goodwill anytime soon. I want to relish the comfort of an old friend.

# 29

## *Ivy*

This morning I woke up to the sound of laughter coming from the kitchen, the kind of laughter that chimes like a chorus of handbells spiritedly playing a jovial tune. It went on for several minutes before I realized I was no longer sleeping and this laughter was real. I looked over at Nolly's cot and saw that it was empty. The sun had not yet risen but the darkness was beginning to surrender to its morning conqueror. I rose from my bed and tiptoed into the dark kitchen slowly trying to discover where the laughter was coming from but more importantly the cause of such merriment at this hour of the morning. I found Nolly on the floor near the stove lying on her back and clutching her stomach while peals of laughter continued. As I looked around the kitchen I saw nothing, or rather no one that might be causing this amusement. The curtains were still drawn in the windows above the sink basin. The door was still tightly shut and bolted. The table was empty of any food or beverage that might have been mysteriously responsible for this mirthful awakening.

I knelt down quietly next to the child because I did not want to alarm or frighten her out of her glee. With eyes squeezed shut she continued to evoke fresh new belly laughs as if in response to some merciless tickling. At this point I believed the child was still sleeping and dreaming of something amusing but this sounded like the kind of laughter the child would make when tickled, though I must confess,

I've not had the time to engage in such sport with Nolly. Listening to laughter of this intensity has the effect of contagion. I began to laugh as well. I had no idea why but in no time we were both laughing hysterically.

Nolly suddenly opened her eyes and looked bewildered. "Why are you laughing, Auntie?" she asked.

I composed myself quickly and replied, "I might ask you the same question. What are you doing at this hour of the morning, alone in the kitchen, laughing so hard?"

"I was remembering."

"Really? What were you remembering? Pray tell!"

Nolly looked at me before speaking. "Well, I guess it's fine to tell you. You are Mommy's sister. When I was a little girl, (which almost made me laugh again) Daddy, Mommy, and I used to play a game. We didn't have the money to do things for real so we pretended. One day we pretended we were going to go to the theater to see a famous show. Daddy said we cannot go to the theater without proper clothes, so, he pulled the sheet and the blanket off the bed. Daddy tied the blanket to his neck and said he had a proper cape. Mommy pulled the sheet around her shoulders and said she had a proper wrap, and they tied the little pillow cover to my neck and said I had the robe of a princess. But, wait, Daddy said, we needed proper hats." Nolly started laughing again. "Daddy took our three wooden bowls from the table and put them on our heads to wear as hats. Oh, we looked so odd, Mommy said. Then Daddy gave me and Mommy a bunch of wildflowers and led us out to the theater. But, it wasn't really a theater, he twirled us around and around until we got dizzy and then he made us sit down. Daddy wiggled and wiggled in front of us holding a long pointy stick and said, look I am the great shake – spear. Because we were still dizzy, Daddy's wiggling seemed even faster. Daddy looked funny. Mommy said Daddy was very clever. I didn't understand it back then but Mommy explained that the man that told lots and lots of stories – his name was Shakespeare, and Daddy was making fun of his name by making himself shake right before our eyes while holding 'spear.' Get it, Auntie? Shake- spear! This morning when I woke up I remembered this and *now* I understand because Daddy was shaking and he was holding a 'spear' and now it's very funny. Don't you think it is funny, Auntie?" I laughed at her delayed understanding of a tender memory. "Yes, Nolly, it is very funny." I kissed the top of her head. "Your Mommy and Daddy are not far away, you know. They are close by and they come to you and still make you laugh."

Nolly grew quiet for a few moments and I was afraid I had spoiled her cheery mood. That memory couldn't have been from too long ago but it was very sweet how the child was still trying to hang on to her happy fragments of memory.

"Nolly, I would like to take you someplace special today. I know I leave the house from time to time to take care of business but today I am not going to take care of business; I want to take you to Charring Cross for a special treat. I'll bet it is something that will make your tongue tickle. Would you like that?"

"Yes, Auntie. What is it?"

"It's a surprise, my love. But, you must promise me to stay in the servants' quarters this morning and be very, very good. I will get my morning chores finished and then we will quickly go to Charring Cross for the treat. Promise me?" She nodded her head but I could see impatience brewing in her eyes. I mustn't delay. I'd been scrimping from my own private allowance to repay my mistress the money that was stolen on Adams St. but I felt that two pennies for a treat would not hurt; there was no way to make up the whole total anyway should the mistress return as planned in just a few weeks. I suppose I needed a treat myself.

To be honest, these past few months since Colleen died have been more difficult than I ever expected. It isn't just the added responsibility of caring for a child, that in and of itself has been a tremendous learning experience. What did I know about children? I was still a child myself when I came into service. Now I have inadvertently stepped into an unfamiliar role and I'm doing the best I can. If I can serve the needs of employers, I can certainly put this talent into raising a child. I fear for what the mistress will say when she returns. I hope that Nolly will listen to the rules more carefully.

What has been troubling me even more than my parental type worries is my personal grief over losing my sister. It is not that Colleen and I were close; I'd only come to know her again when Danny brought her to London a short time ago but I rarely had enough time to visit with her because of all my additional responsibilities here at Mrs. Livingston's once the household staff left around the same period. I believe it is a feeling far greater than loss and grief for parents that I'll never see again, for Killian and the hole in the family heart that he left behind, for Tim and Aidan, and now for Colleen. Not only am I the last of our little family, but I'm the last to remember, to carry the memories of the O'Neill family in my head.

I remember my own Pa coming in from the fields, smelling of earth and rain and grabbing my Ma by the waist and dancing with her in our small cottage to the tune of *O Molly Mine* which he sang entirely off-key, and Killian, Tim, Aidan, and I would sit and laugh just like Nolly at her father's shenanigans. Ma would dance for a moment or two and then she'd remove her apron and swat Pa with it and tell him to go wash that he smelled like Reva, the cow. Us children would then laugh even harder and low at Pa saying, *moo, moo, moo.* He would snatch Ma's apron away from her and begin swatting us with it. Colleen was just a babe in the crib; she wouldn't have remembered. Poor Colleen, she had missed the joyous times our family had together. By the time she was old enough to be aware of the family collage everything had been distorted and we were no longer recognizable as a family. We had each brought a special shape to our beautiful mosaic but now it was lost forever.

Killian was the poet in the family. He wanted to write just like that new poet, Yeats, the one that he'd learned about in school. Most evenings while we sat around the fire, Killian would read us what he'd written that day while taking a break from tilling the soil in the field.

*My words, like single drops of water upon the sea*
*Cannot increase in form, sufficient to remember thee,*
*Thy vapors fade as thy tender voice ebbs far away from me*
*- but love, that current that continues to reminisce of thee...*
*Shall find thee still and pure.*

Who will remember Killian when I no longer can? Why has his voice faded from my mind but the sight of him laid out on his bed still burns within my dreams? Are we all just best forgotten? How long will Nolly continue to retain these memories of her parents? Or does the memory really matter as long as the current of love continues. My heart weighs heavy with the duty to carry the souls of my departed family and the unused love I still feel for all of them.

Charring Cross station is not as crowded today as is normal for a sunny afternoon. Nolly stays close to me, clinging to my side poor thing; she has not left the house much since her mother died and now she is wary of the bustle and commotion. What an obedient child she comported herself to be all morning, playing quietly in the kitchen and shining the table when she sought to please me with her work. Each time I passed the kitchen, however, she asked me "Is it the hour for treats yet?"

At the red and white striped stall in front of the station we arrive like two eager champions eager to claim a prize. Nolly stands on tiptoe trying to see above the counter, wondering still what the surprise could be. A large man with a white hat too tight for his round head leans over the counter and I tell him that we wish to buy two ice creams in a shell. "Vanilla or cinnamon," he asks us. Nolly looks at me with such perplexity and near-panic so I lift her into my arms. "The treat that will tickle your tongue, my sweet, is ice cream and the man must know if you want vanilla or cinnamon."

"I don't know," she replies. "I just don't know." Her bottom lip looked ready to curl down in disappointment.

The man seems to sense her anxiety and offers a solution. "How about a bit of each on your shell, love? And the same for you, Miss? That way you both get to try a little of each." Nolly's lip curves into a smile. I thank the man and pay for our treats. We sit on a nearby bench and lick our ice creams from the shells.

Upon taking her first bite, Nolly jumps off the bench and begins hopping up and down. "Oh, Auntie, it's cold and tickly." I laugh at her bouncing reaction to a simple treat but remind her that she needs to sit on the bench to eat it. Ice cream has a way of melting and dripping onto the ground, then it could no longer be eaten. Fearful of losing her treat, Nolly sits quietly and savors each lick.

"Which do you like better, Auntie, vanilla or cinnin?" she asks me.

"Mmmm, I like them both, I cannot choose. How about you?"

"Me too," she says. I notice that for the first time since her mother died, Nolly is not carrying granny along with her. She hasn't let the statue out of her sight since the greenhouse day, but today I saw her put it on her cot and tuck her in with a blanket before we left. The statue seems to give her comfort. Granny's simple presence gives Nolly the security of something that will not die or leave her behind.

## 30

## *Old Befana*

Sometimes, my mind stretches far back into those early years to that moment when I suddenly crossed the barrier of my tiny existence and reached into a wider range when I became as compliant as the wind. Certainly, my journey began with my own will and my desire to lay eyes upon this child of the caring God, and though my spirit may have breezed through many generations seeking his gentle face, it is the little faces I have encountered along the way that helped me discover who I'm actually looking for. In the beginning, naïve thinking convinced me that I could only find this blessed child in the most extraordinary place or experience, not in the ordinary. It took quite a few thumps of my arthritic knuckles against my thick head to help me realize that the point of familiarity is reached by trust. I believe that is what the three fellas from the east had to their credit; that was how they were able to *see* the star in the first place, they trusted that this was the special star that would lead them to the special child. They didn't have to have proof first; it was trust that made them follow it in the first place.

It was not so much what I had to my own credit that encouraged me to begin on this path, for I had no education, no knowledge; I had nothing, and spiritually I had even less. But also there were no expectations to get in the way of trust. I didn't lead a cluttered life. I was simply *there* when I heard a little message from passersby, and that is all that the caring

God needed from me. It is like being still enough to hear the faint sound that a finger makes as it curls through the silent air beckoning the listener to follow. I wanted to take advantage of this chance to find the baby boy that was born a poor king, this once in a lifetime opportunity to be wanted by someone. Ahh, what a message indeed! Who wouldn't want to hear it? Because *this* baby was born we can all be born into the family of the caring God. He wants every last one of us. Even someone as insignificant as me. Though I've never known why, I've undoubtedly done nothing to merit this invitation but he actually wanted Old Befana as much as he wants everyone else. And that makes me want him too. It's all right if it takes me a long time to get there, and I don't mind the things I need to do along the way even if it hurts because someone so big and caring wants *me*.

In all the time since I dropped my life like a sack of rocks in the middle of a dead end road and followed that star, I haven't regretted one minute. Bit by bit I realized that everyone I have met was someone I was supposed to meet – someone who *could* lead me closer. Oh, believe me there are plenty of people out there that can lead me astray. Too many. I found that out the hard way. When I stopped seeing the star I knew I was headed in the wrong direction. Each new experience, each fresh start has been another step closer as long as I don't lose sight of the star. I have to keep it in front of me.

The star is the sparkle in the eyes of children; when you care about the child, even if it's a child that's grown up, you get a little closer to the caring God. The trick, you see, is to have the eyes to see *the child*. People get older; they work at their jobs, they bring families into the world, they laugh, they cry, they grow old and sit in lonely corners, but the child that wants to know what to do to please someone is still there; the child that needs to feel the strong yet gentle arms of love embrace them lives within each person no matter how old they get. The joy of a child is powerful. The desire to share that youthful joy is as strong as a thunderstorm (and you can't hold back a thunderstorm). All that people really want when they reach a lonely time of life is to gather up youth again and bring it along wherever fate might lead them. Protect the child, I always say. Protect that child within. People that truly know how to love understand that. They know that there is a child inside everyone and whatever you do, you just don't do anything that will wound the child – that's how you know you've gone the wrong way – when you take away the sparkle in the eyes of the child, no matter how old they've gotten. This, my friends, is the greatest injustice there is.

A woman abandoned by a lover, a man cursed by his father, a mother whose maternal care and devotion is repaid with resentment, blame or contempt by her children, an elderly man who has his good name hauled through the mud because of dishonesty, anything that takes the childlike sparkle out of a person's eyes is a grave offense. I might be an Old Befana, not very smart, certainly not pretty, and without a penny to my name, but I have one thing that everyone else has – the power to protect the sparkle. You don't take away a person's sparkle, and if you see it waning you give them some of yours in whatever way you can. It seems easier with children, give them a little treat and watch them light up, but it appears more difficult as they grow older –that's just it, though – it's not! If you can discover the loss, that secret place where the sparkle began to lose its flicker you can replenish it and you'll see them shine like a bright new penny again; you'll see it in their eyes.

# 31

## *Margaret*

I've packed up my belongings and set them out to be carried to the coach. The train does not leave until three this afternoon so I have plenty of time to carry out my scheme. There are three crates sitting on the front veranda ready to be transported to Ulverston and I've hired the boy who comes to care for the lawn and flowers to help me today. Randall seems more than eager to help, either because he enjoys it, or because he needs the extra shillings I pay him each week. I tend to believe it's the latter but no matter what I ask him to do, he consents quite cheerfully. I could take a lesson from young Randall – whatever your lot in life, bear it with good cheer. I know that Randall is the oldest of five children. I know that his father was injured in his fishing boat during a storm and earns very little money now making nets and selling them at the docks. I know that Randall's mother tries to help by taking in laundry (so I send her mine) and I know that his younger sister, Clare, is in the service of housekeeping for I myself have hired her for the summer. I have written a letter of reference for her so that she may find new work once I leave Grange. She tries, poor dear, but she cannot possibly maintain the high standards set by Ivy, that young woman can read my mind!

Randall is packing the crates into the coach without question. He understands that we have an errand to perform before my personal effects are packed onto a later coach. Once we arrive at the nursing home he asks me if he should bring the crates indoors. I explain to him that I must first speak with the head nurse and then I will signal him to bring in the crates.

It takes more time to locate the head nurse, Mrs. Meeks, than I had anticipated. She is on the second floor when I find her and she is quite overwhelmed with a patient suffering from some sort of unsavory delusions. The patient is a woman who is not only taller than Mrs. Meeks but surprisingly stronger. The patient has removed all of her clothing and one can see that there is only a thin veil of flesh that covers her veins and bones. The strong muscles she is using to push three nurses aside are invisible. She wishes to go to the third floor, but there is no third floor in this building, and she is angry that the nurses are trying to stop her. She is shouting, "Let me go, you tyrants. You cannot keep me here. I have an appointment with Sir Anthony Williams-Scott. He is my lover and he is waiting for me on the third floor. He has promised to marry me, now let go of my arms and stand aside. I don't want to go back into that room. I want to go away from here." The nurses are doing all in their power to keep the unruly patient from falling down the stairs to the first floor. Finally, one of the nurses shouts above the din, "Yes, Miss Alisha, okay. I'm going to take you away from these other nurses. You are right. They are tyrants. Let me take you to the third floor; first, we'll wash you up and put on a pretty gown, then you can wait for Sir Anthony in your bed. Alright? Calm yourself, now. He is coming." The woman stops fighting and surrenders to the clever nurse and follows her directions. The scene has quite given me a newfound admiration for the work these women do.

When Mrs. Meeks finally reaches me at the bottom of the stairs she is disheveled and an air of annoyance still lingers. I ask her permission to bring a few gifts into Bess Whitney's room and Mrs. Meeks gives me a dismissive wave and says of course, go on then. I signal to Randall to begin bringing in the first of the crates (the one marked with a 1) and he follows me down the corridor into Aunt Bess's room. She is not by her window today but still in her nightgown and in bed. The bed next to hers is now empty and the woman by the door who lies on her side and stares at nothing is still doing so as if she hasn't budged a muscle since my last visit.

Aunt Bess sees me enter and immediately sits up and fusses with her gown, her hair, and her covers, trying to affect a presentable appearance.

"I'm so sorry, Aunt Bess, I should have sent word that I was coming to see you today. Please forgive me."

"Nonsense, dear, come in, come in. I thought you were going back to London today. It's so good to see you, Margaret."

I kiss her on each cheek as she'd taught me to do so long ago. "I am leaving on the three o'clock train, Aunt Bess, but I wanted to stop by for a visit first and if it is alright, I have brought you a little something." Signaling to Randall who is standing just outside the door with crate number 1, I ask Aunt Bess if it's okay with her to help her into a new robe I've brought her.

"Oh, my, you didn't have to do that." But, she is smiling largely. I open crate number 1 and nod my head to Randall to bring in crate number 2. While he is out, I take the robe out of the crate and unfold it. Aunt Bess gasps. It is a robe of pure silk, a deep rich crimson with a trim of gold beading.

"Oh, Margaret, what have you done?"

"You'll see, Aunt Bess." I help her into her new robe and take the earrings made of ringlets of red glass from the crate and help her put them in her ears. She starts laughing. "I didn't have a sari but I thought this would do," I tell her. She can't speak; she just laughs. Then I brush her hair back and hold it in place with a beautiful comb made of golden beads. I remove the makeup case from the crate and give her a small red dot in the middle of her forehead, pencil some ebony liner along the edges of her eyelids and paint her lips a dark shade of red. I hold a hand mirror in front of her so she can see how absolutely beautiful she looks. Her hands go up to her cheeks. "Oh, Margaret," is all she can manage to say while a dew of tears settles into her eyes.

Just then, Randall walks in with crate number 2. Aunt Bess's eyes widen. "What more could there be?" From crate number 2 I remove layers of silken fabrics in all colors and textures. I begin to drape them around the window, along the sides of her bed and chair, and then with permission from her roommates I cover their beds in silk as well. When crate number 3 arrives I take the small palm plant and place it on the bedside stand next to Aunt Bess's bed.

Through glistening eyes she says, "It's India." Next, I take out a Chimpta set and place them into her hands; they are fire tongs with brass jingles so that she can make music. She nearly screeches with delight. "Where did you get these?"

"You gave them to me after you'd finished turning your house into the Taj Mahal, Aunt Bess. I still had them, though I did have to do some searching through the attic of the summer house to find them. Finally, I found them under a box of Mary's disused gowns and I wanted you to have them and enjoy." She shakes them and laughs; the clatter is so inviting that the woman in the bed who only lays on her side and stares blankly suddenly sits up and gapes at us like she is dreaming. The others gawk at us, too.

All at once I feel something bristle inside my heart, something I have not felt in such a long time. Aunt Bess reaches out her arms to me. I sit on the bed next to her and nearly slip to the floor because of the silk. I lean over and accept her embrace. Her laughter has now subsided and turns to tears. "Do you have any idea how happy you've made me today, Margaret?"

"It was you who introduced this kind of happiness into my own starched and boring life." At that she throws back her head and laughs again. "Your parents were really stuffed shirts weren't they?"

I laugh as well. "Yes, well, father anyway. Mother was such a dear and tried her best with us but it was a challenge for her to keep up with him. I'm glad I was able to do today just a fraction of what you did for me." Aunt Bess shakes her head. "No. I'm fine. You need to do something for *you*." She pokes her finger sharply into my chest. "Get your happiness back, my dear. Do something to get it back. Promise me? I know darn well that life isn't fair, that people run out on us and hurt us; that the unimaginable can happen and break us apart, but you can't surrender to that, my dear. Take hold and make a choice to be happy again."

I feel the dam within me swelling and ready to burst; I want to leave now, to catch my train back to London. Sensing my need to escape, she hurries to continue, "Do you think that my life was all gaiety and charm?" I don't look up or reply. "I was happy because I decided I wanted to be, not because sad things didn't enter my life, and not because I wasn't completely devastated from time to time. You were too young to know what happened in between all the parties and frivolity. I thought I was going to die from a broken heart, Margaret." I don't think I want to hear this. I just want to leave. "George and I, we wanted children. It's not that I couldn't conceive. I conceived many times; I simply couldn't bring the children to term. My little loves died inside of me time and time again and each time they took a piece of me with them. But each time I had to decide once again to just keep going. I had to overcome the fear that without a family of my own there was no one to love, that there was nothing to live for. Please, Margaret, please don't give up on happiness. Sometimes you'll find that if you can make just one other person happy, you find your own joy in there somewhere."

"I'm unable..." I begin but cannot continue. I just want to get away. Aunt Bess pats my cheek then hugs me fiercely. "I know, my dear, I know. I know." This is my chance to weep but I cannot for I fear that if I begin I will never be able to stop. I want to board the train right now, to escape once again. "Listen to me," she continues. "and then I will let you go. I know you want to get to your train. I thank you from the bottom of my heart for all this joy today. You will never know how much it has meant to me. But this joy that you brought to me today was born out of a longing I had long ago. You carried it with you all these years and brought it back to me. Don't leave here with the intention of remaining closed. When you see that chance to heal, grab it!"

"Thank you, Aunt Bess," I reply quickly and stand up. "I will consider your advice. I promise. I will be back to see you again when I return to Grange. Keep well, yes?" She looks so vulnerable in her new robe surrounded by sheets of silk, palm plants and a Chimpta. If I were in her shoes right now would any of this had made me happy? I kiss her good-bye and turn to leave. The lady in the bed who is always turned on her side toward the door staring at nothing looks at me and waves. I could be mistaken but she looks like she is smiling. They all look so ridiculous in that room, and happy to be so.

# 32

## *Ivy*

At least a dozen times today I looked for something I needed and could not find it. At first I began to believe that my mistress's impending return was making me so jumpy that I was misplacing my broom, my buckets, my cleaning cloths, the basket of linens to be laundered, and even the soap bar and washing board. However, when I found my cleaning cloths inside flower pots, and the soap in the kitchen sideboard with the flour and sugar, my buckets on the outdoor patio, the garden rake inside the study and my broom lying on the piano bench, I knew I wasn't losing my faculties because of my own forgetfulness; I had some help. I caught a glimpse of my impish niece taking the umbrellas out of their stand in the front hall and planting them in a straight line in the garden and tying some satin ribbon from one to the next creating a decorative enclosure for her borrowed "treasures."

Mrs. Livingston is expected to arrive next week. It will be a bit later than she normally returns for it will be October already rather than the first of September by the time her coach arrives. Though I have had extra time to prepare for her arrival many chores must wait until the week before, such as putting fresh linens on her bed and making sure that each room of her living quarters is in finest form. My chest tightened with anxiety as I watched Nolly arranging several books from the study in her own manufactured bookcase on the patio made from overturned buckets and wooden planks.

She is a creative child, but what am I to do? These activities will be grossly unacceptable when my mistress returns.

When Nolly came into the kitchen to snatch additional towels for her "curtains," I purposely stood in the entryway blocking her passage with my body. With my arms folded across my chest and a stern look of disapproval painted on my face; I did not budge until she spoke.

"Auntie, you are in my way – say excuse me."

I did not move, and I did not speak. I wanted to grasp her full attention. It was time to nip this behavior in the bud. She tried to get past me to my right and then to my left. I stood firm. Finally, in an exasperated tone she said,

"Auntie, you are being quite naughty. This is not a fun game. Please move aside; you are keeping me from my chores." At that, I seized the opportunity to reply,

"You do not like it when I am naughty?" She shook her head, no.

"You do not like it when I keep you from your chores?" Again, she shook her head.

"You do not like it when I play games that are fun for me, but not for you?" She made no response. "Come with me, child and sit in the chair while we review the rules." I turned to walk toward the table and chairs. I looked to see if she was behind me but she had turned and run out of the door once again. My jaw dropped. I saw through the glass that she had run all the way to the other side of the garden and then threw herself down to the ground. My first instinct was to charge out there and lead her back inside for a more serious talk about not only disobedience but disrespectfulness, too. Had she acted this way with Colleen? What would my sister have done in this situation? I can't leave her out there like that unattended, and I don't wish to force her back into the house like an ill-behaved pet. I have so much to do I don't even feel like I have time to think this through. If I had acted like this with my parents... Pa would have sent me to the shed without dinner. It was harsh, but...

I stepped outside the door. I saw that granny was sitting on a perch that Nolly had made specifically for the statuette. A large crate was covered with a damask buffet coverlet from the dining room. I exhaled loudly. Two silver candlesticks stood on each side. I had an idea.

Standing over Nolly at the far end of the garden, I stated in a very calm voice that granny would like to have a word with her and that she needed to come into the kitchen at once. At those words, Nolly stood up straight. She had not been crying; she simply looked angry. I turned and led the way toward the house. This time Nolly followed. In the kitchen, granny sat plainly on the table but immediately I sat closest to the statue and signaled for Nolly to sit at the farther end. She kept her eyes intently on the statue and would not look at me.

I began with, "Granny says that she enjoys spending time with you but she needs you to remember some things."

"First of all," I continued, "it's not nice to take things that belong to other people. Granny knows that you have taken many, many things that do not belong to you. She sees you and she knows that even though you are only borrowing these things, you have never asked for permission. That is a very important part of borrowing." Nolly seemed to be listening (not to me, of course.)

"Secondly, it is very upsetting to granny when she is made a party to your disobedient behavior. It makes her feel uncomfortable and worried because she does not want you to get hurt or into trouble."

"Thirdly, granny has advised me that if you continue to disobey, to take things without permission, to go into places where you are not allowed, or to act defiantly when you are asked to do something, there will be consequences. You will be confined to the bedchamber until you can learn to obey."

"Finally, when the mistress returns next week, granny must remain with her at *all* times. If you wish to visit granny, you must obtain the mistress's permission through me – your auntie." At this final stipulation, Nolly put her small fists into her eye sockets to push back the tears that wanted to spill forth.

"Granny wants to know if you understand. Nod your head if you understand." Nolly nodded her head. "Now, granny wants you to put everything back, nice and clean and tidy just as you found them and if you don't you must go to the bedchamber at once." I clapped my hands to indicate that she should begin at once. I added, "And granny is to remain right here on this table until you are finished. She wants to make sure that you do as she has asked."

Nolly began at once to comply with my demands. Why hadn't I thought of using a surrogate disciplinarian before now? Then again, how long would this method prove effective?

# 33

## *Margaret*

Outside the window of the train the English landscape is a picture postcard that repeats itself regularly: rolling green pastures, grazing flocks of sheep, antiquated farmhouses, picturesque villages, hedges and streams near gravel lanes, delicate wildflowers, and then repeat. The scene never tires; it offers as much beauty with each repetition as a young maiden who, upon rising each morning, adorns herself skillfully when presenting herself to suitors. The train ambles steadily along through Leeds, over the river Trent, crossing through Nottingham, and keeping its pace through Aylesbury before reaching the London Station at King's Cross. Though it is quite late when I reach the station, I had wired ahead to have a coach waiting and it is Mr. Sharp again who is here to greet and assist me upon my arrival. Since I have been making these biannual sojourns alone in the past couple of years I have found comfort in consistency, and placing myself in Mr. Sharp's care. It will be nearly midnight by the time I arrive home but I know that Ivy will be waiting – I don't know what I would do without her.

I have brought her a small token of appreciation from this hiatus. I have never done so before, but for some reason this time I felt compelled to do so. I saw this trinket and it simply reminded me of her. It is a small cherry wood music box with an oval engraving of an Irish village at the center of the lid. Its simplicity struck me at once, just like Ivy, but it was the melody that plays upon opening the box that brought her to mind. *Let Erin Remember...* The tune tinkles delicately for a few bars and then repeats.

*Let Erin remember the days of old...*
*Thus shall memory often in dreams sublime*
*Catch a glimpse of the days that are over*
*Thus sighing, look through the waves of time*
*For the long-faded glories they cover.*

Ivy always sings this tune as she dusts each room of the house. I believe it is the only song she knows for I have never heard her sing another. I think I will give her this little box for Christmas this year. Perhaps I will find a small trifle to put inside it as well. I could not have found a more faithful and devoted servant than Ivy O'Neill.

The coach stops in front of my home and Mr. Sharp takes my bags up to the front door. As expected, Ivy must have been waiting by the window in the front in the front hall for she opens the door as soon as we arrive and helps Mr. Sharp with my bags. There is a brisk wind tonight and it nearly snatches my hat from my head. Quickly I duck into the house and pay Mr. Sharp his fee plus a handsome gratuity for his consistent service. He smiles broadly and thanks me, nearly skipping his way back to the coach. As Ivy helps me with my cloak and hat I notice that she looks extremely tired and worn. It is odd; normally she looks refreshed when I return home as if her duties have been lightened by my absence. Tonight she seems quite anxious.

"All is well, I hope, Ivy?" I ask.

She nods. "Oh yes, Ma'am. All is well. You must be quite tired from your journey. It has been quite a long day for you, I trust. Your room is ready and there is a small fire to take the chill out of the air. The wind is causing quite a draft this night."

"Yes, this old house is horribly drafty, but I trust that there have been no problems out of the ordinary."

"All is well, Ma'am." But there is something about the firmness with which she speaks tonight that causes me some concern.

"I am quite certain that you are tired, as well, Ivy. If there are no matters of urgency let's both of us retire for the night. We shall speak tomorrow." She hands me my usual cup of warm milk and plate of my favorite peppermints. She never fails me.

## 34

## *Old Befana*

It always makes me roll my eyes when I hear people say things like "I'm amazed by how disrespectful some of the younger generation can be to their elders these days. Why when I was that age I never..." Hah! I want to tell them, at that age you were even worse! The past becomes some sort of a polished souvenir like one of those glass balls filled with water, artificial snow, and a scene of dubious perfection frozen in time. They like to shake the ball and watch the fluttery snowflakes; it makes them smile and they do it again. But inside the ball is the truth they've all forgotten – it's COLD, the sun rarely shines, and there is no hope that anything will change.

There was a woman named Decima that lived in a big house down the lane from me in my old home town. She and I had known each other for quite some time but we weren't exactly friends. I didn't have any friends because I didn't know how to be one. She didn't have many friends because she couldn't stop talking. Yet, somehow we were always thrown together. I couldn't get to the well in the center of town without passing in front of her house; that was the problem. It was the first of my problems. So, at least two or three times a day when I had to fetch a new crock of water I had to encounter Decima Bucca (that was her nickname: *ten times the mouth of one*) no matter how quietly I tried to pass by her house. She seemed to be watching for me. Didn't she ever have anything better to do, I always wondered? Didn't that big old house of hers need some cleaning? She'd catch me coming and going. I think she just wanted someone to listen. Well, I have a good set of ears.

It was always the same kind of story. "You know," she'd say, "whenever someone asks me for something I give it to them. Do they say thank you, or do anything for me? No, they don't."

Then, don't give them anything, I'd tell her. "I tell people when I see them that they are looking fine, today. Do they ever tell me I'm looking fine? Never." Then don't tell them they look fine, I offered. "These younger people these days, when you talk to them, they don't listen. If you try to give them good advice they laugh in your face." Then, don't give them good advice, I'd remind her. "Maledicta," she'd curse, "why do I even bother trying to talk?" Please stop talking, I'd tell her, but she wouldn't hear me for she continued on. Now I know I should have encouraged her.

Decima's favorite lament was that young people did not have the intellect of a *mus* (that would be a mouse). If someone told them that eating Amanita mushrooms would make them turn into the pharaohs of Egypt they would eat them twenty times a day. 'The problem with youth is the endless wanting and no regrets about doing." I'd sigh. "And the problems with us old ladies," I'd tell her "is that wanting is a thing of the past. And we regret many things." But she didn't hear me. She never did.

For as long as I must wander the earth in search of that little miracle who was born to heal us, I will never forget the reason for some of my bitterness back then. It all has to do with regrets. As a very young woman I had so little in the way of social experience. I always used to say, "For Jupiter's sake, if I could only begin to understand people I might actually like them and want to talk to them." But I never sympathized with a single soul, or maybe what I thought I understood about them sent me burrowing inwardly more deeply than before. What I have learned now is that understanding is not always like a sudden light that comes on, it's more like waking up slowly from a deep sleep. I spent all my time in my hometown sound asleep as if Morpheus himself was keeping me from ever waking up.

Lethargy coupled with a sense of pride combined to cause my biggest regret. I didn't want to see certain truths about people or about myself because I was foolhardy enough to think that I already understood; I'd made judgments and I was certainly vindicated in my way of thinking. It was the time when a stray gaggle of mountain boys, probably an Alpine tribe, found their way south. They weren't acting under any official direction or commands; they'd simply splintered off in search of their own personal victories. They came through my hometown and because of its remoteness; they liked it and decided to stay. They weren't a very nice bunch, I'll tell you that. Some of the villagers decided to fight back but all we had were garden tools whereas these rogue young soldiers had real weapons and they wanted to take our homes and our women and burn our village to the ground if we resisted. It's the kind of thing that happens when you haven't invited trouble – it just shows up. When I saw them I brought my chickens inside along with some food and shuttered my windows and bolted my door. But they weren't interested in my shabby little hovel (the advantage of living in a one-room hut); they were much more interested in the bigger houses like Decima's, Claudio's, and that rich fella on the hill whose name I never knew.

When I peeked through the slit in my shutter I saw that this group of quasi-soldiers was nothing but a mob of very young adolescents. They were twelve, thirteen years old but they were big ones! Their size betrayed their age, but they had seen war so they weren't unsullied, just frightening. They had the experiences of seasoned men grappling inside the minds of children. Things like war are adult business but these were still just kids and the adults they'd known thought it was a good idea to train them early on. Do you know what happens when you pressure children to grow up too fast and *force* them into adulthood? I didn't understand the madness of it all back then; I wish I had. These children were told, *well, you're going to have to face war sooner or later so you might as well be equipped to deal with it now. Here is your bow, here is your arrow, here is your spear, this is how you use them; now go out and fight. This is what you do to men when they get in your way. This is what you do to women if you should want one, and worst of all, this is what you do to their children, you can sell them and fund your triumphs. You might as well learn it while you're young, even if your poor soul is not ready to cope with the consequences; if you should get into trouble, kiss a normal life good-bye – that's the way it is.* These youths had bought the indoctrination they'd received but they were tired of taking orders from adults who treated them like children one minute and expected them to live up to adult responsibilities the next, so they'd set off on their own.

There were a lot of them and their leader seemed to be an untamed youth called Alessandro. He couldn't have been more than fourteen years old but he was the size of a cistern and strong as the scirocco wind at full gale force. He seemed to plow right through grown men of equal size like they were nothing more than young stalks of wheat in an open field. He commanded obedience from his youthful followers through fear and intimidation. They all duplicated his fierce manner. They'd been taught to bully others into their ways of thinking. He led them all into fierce attacks against our naïve villagers, clubbing the men, breaking into homes, stealing food, and pillaging whatever they could find. Finally, the man on the hill whose name I cannot remember came down to offer the young soldiers a deal. He told them that if they assembled in the town square at dusk and halted their attacks against the villagers he would gather all his riches and bring them to the square during the night. He told them they were wasting their time plundering the poor, they should wait for the real loot and they were free to take it all and abandon this village forever. The naïve youths agreed. The man from the hill told them to sit together in the middle of the square and wait until all the sacks of riches were brought to them. If they tried to take them before he was finished, they would miss out on the most valuable pieces which would come at the very end. So, the youths complied. They huddled together in the middle of the town square while all the villagers brought loaded sacks and placed them in a circle around the soldiers. If you recall the main resource in my hometown was well-seasoned compost and animal droppings. Well, that was what was in the sacks. Alessandro and many of the youths had fallen asleep while huddled together waiting for all the sacks to arrive – they'd had a busy day of raiding. When the circle of sacks was complete the men of the town used their torches and set fire to all the sacks. The circle went up in a tremendous blaze. The sleeping youths, including Alessandro, had no time to escape the infernal trap. A few of the younger boys dove through the flames but were attacked by the angry village men. One youth, however, managed to dodge the attackers and ran down the street, right up to my little house. He began banging on the door crying for help. I peeked through the slit in my shutters. I saw his terrified face, the look of fear in his eyes. He was just a child. I had the chance to help him but I did not. I had to make my own fear bigger than his so I didn't have to help him. Sometimes the greatest dangers are not outside our homes, banging on our doors; quite often the greatest danger is the fear within our own hearts. This tremendous fear keeps us apart from each other and from doing good. I found out something about myself that night that I didn't like and then I had to hide it from myself so I wouldn't see it. That night, I couldn't help a child. I thought he would hurt me if I let him in. I will regret that moment for all of my days. I sat in the corner of my hut and cried for that child. I cried for his mother. I cried for the life he could have had or should have had. When I finished crying I stood up and ran to open the door to let him in but by the time I reached the door it was too late. It was too late. Sooner or later we all do something that we're sorry about and sometimes it's irreparable.

# 35

## Ivy

Even a wink of sleep during the night would have been useful but I tossed around in my bed like a drop of water in a skillet of oil. At one point I nearly fell out of bed and gasped loud enough to wake up Nolly. The poor child, I must have frightened her, she crawled into my bed and huddled into the nook of my arm. At that point I couldn't move at all for fear of waking her even more. I gave up on sleep. I rehearsed my explanation to my mistress for the funds that went missing the day I went to the bank. The terror which I felt was not about Mrs. Livingston's reaction; she has always been very kind to me and has often overlooked my imperfections. It is my own feelings of not wanting to disappoint the woman who has been so good to me. How do I tell her something I feel so ashamed of? I wish there was a way she didn't have to know, but of course she will know and she won't be angry because she is so patient, but what I have to offer to make amends is insufficient. How can I possibly make up for my own inadequacy to a woman who has been so benevolent, even in allowing my sister and niece to live here?

When morning finally comes I am up earlier than usual. Nolly eventually took over most of my bed and bedcovers. I pray she remembers our talk from yesterday. *The mistress of the house is coming home. You may only present yourself to her or in the living quarters if she permits you. You must replace the statue where you found her, and you must never remove anything without asking me first. I will ask the mistress personally. Do you understand?* Nolly has been so obedient since the day we had a talk with granny's help. She told me yesterday not to worry, Auntie, she would be very good and follow the rules. She even smiled as she said it as if this had been her plan all along. She seemed to sense my anxiety but her words did little to allay my fears. I knew how quickly she could forget her promises. I steeled myself for my own admission of guilt to the lady of the house. I prepared Mrs. Livingston's favorite tea and sweet bread for breakfast and arranged a tray to take to her room. For Nolly, I left some of the sweet bread and a cup of milk with honey on the nightstand between our beds and a carton of old clothing scraps on the floor for her to play dress-up after her breakfast. This activity seemed to occupy her for hours, especially in front of the looking glass. Please, Lord, I need a chance to do what needs to be done without any complications.

It wasn't until mid-morning that my mistress sent for me in her study. I had hoped to speak with her sooner but I had to endure a morning of fretfulness as I had passed the entire night. Nolly stayed in our bedchamber, as far from me as she could get. I couldn't blame the child; I was composed of very sharp edges this morning. I entered the study upon Mrs. Livingston's summons.

"Come in, Ivy, sit please," she began. "We have much to discuss. How is everything? Once again I must tell you how much I appreciate your steadfast management of my home and affairs while I was away. It is gratifying to know that you are able to manage so well."

"Ma'am, I must tell you… First of all, I hope your time at Grange was restful for you. You look well. Very well, Ma'am! I feel that I must tell you…"

"Did something happen, Ivy? Please bring me up to date. My goodness, you're trembling. What is it?"

I took a deep breath and I didn't take another until I had explained the entire ordeal of the stolen funds. I put my hands to my face to steady my emotions but Mrs. Livingston immediately told me to calm myself. She said she understood my anxiety and she was dreadfully sorry that I had had to experience such a violation of my person. She told me I should have written to tell her so that she could send a message to Mr. Trumble to authorize more funds...

"Oh, no, Ma'am. I wish to pay you back for the deficit out of my earnings. It is only right that I should do so, Ma'am."

My mistress heaved a huge sigh. She did not wish to agree but she sensed that it would somehow help me feel better. "We'll discuss it after I have had some time to think about it, Ivy. For now, put it out of your mind. I must confess, you seem much more distressed than this incident should warrant. Are you certain that there is nothing else that is causing you such concern? Is everything well with your sister, Ivy? I recall that just before I left she was ill and came to live here? Has she recovered?"

It was at that moment that my repressed grief suddenly found its opening and I began to cry, not wailing mind you, not in front of my mistress, but softly as if I could only allow a few drops of grief to be released at a time. I told her about Colleen's passing shortly after her departure. She recoiled in her chair at my words and for several moments she did not speak.

"She had a small child, didn't she?" she asked in nearly a whisper. "What of the child?"

I looked up carefully, still trying to avoid her eyes. "She is here, Ma'am. My niece has been staying with me in my quarters and helping me in her own small way. I didn't know what else..."

"I see," she whispered again. "Surely, you did not intend this to be a permanent arrangement Ivy?"

"No, Ma'am, I suppose not, but I did not know what else to do. She is just a small child."

"You have no other family? The child's father?"

"Ma'am, I am all she has."

"Ivy, you do see how this presents a problem?" I did see the problem, on so many levels, even those of which we cannot speak. Mrs. Livingston was generous enough to allow my sister to come here to convalesce but she was supposed to take her child and go home when she felt better. The child remaining here was never part of the agreement. I knew this, but Mrs. Livingston has made it clear; she does not wish to be disturbed when she is away unless it is a matter of urgency.

"Ivy," she'd found her voice now. "Your niece, she is how old?"

"She is four, Ma'am, soon to be five."

"Ah, well, there it is. Tomorrow I shall make certain inquiries. We will find a suitable institution, well... a school which boards children in her circumstances and she can live in a more appropriate environment and receive an education. She will be with other children and find activities which suit one of such a tender age. Surely, it could not have been easy for you during this time to attend to all your duties and care for a child as well?"

I shook my head but I could not respond. Send Nolly away? I had not even thought of that as a possibility. How will Nolly react to being sent away? How will she cope with such losses at *such a tender age*?

"I'm so terribly sorry about your sister, Ivy." That was all that she could say on the subject at this point. It was all a terrible dilemma, of course I'd always known it would be. I simply did not wish to think about it until I had to. This house with all its losses and sorrows. I never thought I would experience my own bereavement within these walls, but sending Nolly away was never an option I had considered.

# 36

## *Margaret*

In the past few days that I have been bringing all of my business affairs up to date and looking into homes for orphaned children, I have not heard a single sound which suggests that there is a four year-old child in this house. Ivy continues to perform all her duties, prepares pleasant meals and keeps everything in my home in perfect order, as usual. Surely, she isn't locking the child up in a cupboard during the day? Ivy, more than anyone, understands my current need for tranquility and she has always worked to make sure that nothing disturbs me. The same cannot be said for my sister Mary today.

"So, the rich and prodigal daughter returns. Did you enjoy your sojourn to… where was it now? Oh yes, our other house, the one in Grange-Over-Sands – it is nearly as large as this one, is it not? My, what does one solitary person do with so many large houses?"

"Mary, what do you want? Really, I have many matters to attend to. Yes, I have been away a bit longer than usual so you must understand that there are other things which concern me at the moment other than your childish laments."

"I am quite certain you have much to deal with, dear sister. I don't know how you manage it all. It must be a tremendous burden to manage the entire family fortune."

"Do you honestly believe I wish to reprise the same old conversation with you, Mary? What do you want from me?

You have a home. You have a husband. You have children. You have sufficient money. Why can't you leave me in peace? That is all I want and that is the one thing you continue to deny me."

"Yes, yes, yes. You want peace. And you want this house, and that house, and you want to be left alone. You are practically a recluse, Margaret. Everyone is talking. You remain withdrawn to this house or to the one in Grange. You refuse visitors. You've stopped attending parties and volunteering at the soup kitchen. And you refuse to respond to David's solicitations."

How is that last statement in particular any of her business? It is always Mary who is so adept at provoking me into raising my voice. "What I do or choose not to do is no one, *no one's* business but my own. Do you understand that? If I wish to cut myself off from everything it is my right to do so. This house and the other – they are just places, nothing more. How I live my life in any place is no one's affair, especially not yours. Now, please, leave me be. Go back to your family and stop meddling in my life."

Mary is not satisfied until she has spent an hour, at least, needling me into a corner from which I must come out defending myself, explaining my actions or pleading for peace. It is like a game for her and she must always win. It matters not how much self-control I try to maintain, the game is not over until she receives the reaction she is seeking – my breakdown. Then she wins, then I am humiliated, then she departs with self-satisfaction. It is never the adversary who is at fault, it is always the responder. I am the one who must recover and restore myself to a calm state. It is I who must feel remorse for my response. Mary knows no other way to relate. I do, and I am the one who fails to rise above the fray. Today, I have the most overwhelming notion that our little tirade was performed before an unseen audience. I know that Ivy is out, but her shadow must be lurking somewhere. I sense that the little one is nearby though I cannot see her at the moment. She must have heard the shouting – my shouting – for Mary always remains aloof when riling me. Perhaps I frightened the poor child. I believe I will ask Ivy to bring the child in to see me. I would like to see her before she leaves, but not today. I must regain my composure. I must reestablish my bearings.

## 37

## *Old Befana*

There is a subtle tension in this home since Margaret returned that hums through the air like a small insect. It travels from room to room gathering energy from each inhabitant: Ivy, who is struggling with the idea of sending Nolly away; Nolly, who suspects that her status in the home has changed dramatically since the mistress's return but cannot understand the nature of her fear, and Margaret whose decision to maintain an obscure existence is being challenged on several fronts, but mostly from within.

As for Ivy, she remembers that when she left Ireland she had wanted to find work in England. Now she is trying to remember if that was all there ever was to her aspirations at fourteen. She lives for her employer; she has not necessarily abandoned any personal dreams because she does not recall ever having any. She remembers loving her family with all her heart but she simply did not want to live in Wicklow without a way to keep a roof over her head and food in her stomach, but had she ever entertained the idea of a home and family of her own? Maybe she allowed fear to talk her out of such a dream. She takes one day at a time and serves the needs of her mistress because she knows no other way of life. Certainly, when she began working for this home, it was a different lifestyle altogether. There were many more servants at that time because there were many more masters. Mr. Barrington's butler, Jacob Knotts, had been the one to hire her. Mr.

Barrington was quite ill at that time and had died a year later. Mrs. Barrington was doing her best to finish raising her three daughters alone.

Margaret and Mary were always bickering while Anne kept to herself. Within three years' time, each of the Barrington ladies had found a decent husband. Anne left for distant lands with her husband, Matthew; Mary took up residence with her husband Niles on the other side of town and gave birth to three children, one right after another. Margaret was the last to wed and her life has been anything but idyllic, but Ivy has had such a soft spot for Margaret, perhaps for the very reason that she was brave no matter what happened. Ivy helped Margaret nurse her mother after her sisters left home and her mother became depressed. She refused to marry David until she felt she could devote herself to him entirely. Her mother needed her and that was her first priority at the time. When Mrs. Barrington passed away so tragically, Margaret and David were later married in a quiet ceremony unlike Mary and Anne's more lavish nuptials.

As for Margaret, it's my opinion that the peace she seeks is impossible to find because of the wounds that she still carries. It is one thing to be *at peace* while it is quite another to live in loneliness. The two are not the same. Her tension comes from bracing herself too tightly preparing for the next blow. Losing her mother affected Margaret in ways she did not expect. Learning of the accident that curtailed the life of a once vibrant, caring, and pious mother shook her foundations about life. Is this what it all came down to, she'd wondered. Roslyn Barrington had been a model for motherhood. Rather than relying on tutors and governesses for her daughters, she spent time with them each day in the study reading to her children and teaching them to read. When the twins were just toddlers, Roslyn converted an entire room into a playroom for the girls and she would spend hours in there with them each day, playing with them and nurturing their growth. The servants were meant to care for the large house, not for her children. Roslyn Barrington had no wish to be a mere spectator in the lives of her children. Margaret had devoted herself to her mother's care as faithfully as Roslyn had dedicated herself to motherhood. When Roslyn died, a part of Margaret's heart went with her, but she vowed that if she ever had children of her own she would follow her mother's example.

As for Nolly, she has been doing what most small children do when they lose a parent at such a young age – she has put her grief up on a shelf next to grownup things like falling in love, problem-solving, and decision-making. She lives her little life in a world of imagination where she enjoys the oddities in life that make her laugh, the perplexing things that make her cry, and the responsibility of figuring out adult expectations of her behavior. She has stayed in the back servant quarters of the house, not so much because of obedience to her auntie but because of fear of the grand mistress who blew into the house like a blustery chill when she returned from the sea. Nolly has been secretively curious about this lady her auntie works so hard to please. She can see the advantages of serving such a great lady if only to live in a house like this, but Nolly wonders whether Ivy simply has no one else to care about. Even when the mistress wasn't here, her auntie went about frantically performing her duties the same as she has since the woman's return. The child is wondering if she could care for her auntie in the same manner that Ivy cares for Mrs. Livingston. The moment of wonder passes quickly, however, when the child's own desires take the forefront of her thoughts. Today, despite her unease and her promises, she wishes to play in the hall that separates the servants' quarters from the main part of the house. She dare not go upstairs again to visit the magical room but there are things she can do to arrange a proper play area that should disturb no one.

Having removed two washboards from the kitchen, a set of washing linens for curtains and an assortment of utensils, Nolly sets up a small haven underneath the service table in the hallway surrounding herself with barriers to the outside world. Here she is safe and not in anyone's way, so she begins to chatter to herself in the way that children do and occasionally laughing at her own silliness. Margaret, who is across the hall in the study hears the childish prattle and finds that she can no longer concentrate on her correspondence. In the weeks since her return the neglected stack of journals, newspapers, and assorted memos, notes, and communications from various sources on her desk have beckoned. She has decided that she ought to tackle them today. There is also an envelope with familiar handwriting which suggests David has tried to contact her once again. She puts this envelope at the very bottom of the pile and prioritizes the remainder of the mail but is suddenly distracted by an explosion of giggles coming from the hallway. Resolutely, she stands up, straightens her clothing and calls for Ivy. Without delay Ivy is at hand and once Margaret states that it is difficult to contemplate the business before her because of certain small noises coming from the hall outside the study, Ivy assures her that the matter will be dealt with expediently. When Ivy leaves the room, the noise stops immediately and Margaret sets the stacks of mail to the side. Now that she has interrupted a child at play and silenced the rare sounds of joy she finds that she is no longer motivated to attend to these matters. She walks over to the window and stares at the abandoned garden with eyes that refuse to blink.

# 38

## *Ivy*

"Come here, my love. I have a task for you. Would you like to help me make some pastries that my mistress loves so dearly? I need you to use this scalloped-edged cutter like this... and push it carefully into the dough until you can feel the table. Can you do that?" Nolly nods her head and presses perfect little flower-like shapes out of dough that is to be baked as tarts. On this late October day, the chill in the air is warmed by the very thought of sweet tarts made with jam.

"Oh dear, let's tie back your unruly hair, shall we? You don't want jam to get into your lovely little curls. It will be a frightening mess if you do." When the pastries come out of the oven, Nolly's task is to take a small spoonful of elderberry jam and place it on top of the tart. The little pastries will go back into the oven for just a few minutes so that the jam sticks nicely to the tarts. Suddenly she exclaims, "I think granny would like us to put a pinch of cocoa in the tarts; just a pinch!" For a moment I am alarmed. "Granny is still in the study with the mistress, correct?"

"Oh, yes," Nolly replies. "She's keeping an eye on the mistress. She thinks she can use a pinch of cocoa to make her happier." We add a pinch of cocoa to each tart. Nolly licks her fingers between each spoonful of jam for it takes two fingers to push the jam off of the spoon and onto the dough. I cannot help but smile at this child.

The bell rings from the study. "I must go see what my mistress wants. You are the supreme guardian of the tarts, my love. Do not let anyone touch them or eat them! Do you understand? We must guard them carefully so that we can put them on a tray and I shall take them to Mrs. Livingston. You are in charge!" Nolly has one finger in her mouth and a bit of sticky dribble running down the sides of her chin. Her eyes are wide and I know she is taking the charge of duty quite seriously but will she be able to resist the temptation to eat a tart while I am gone? I look at her sternly and she nods her head in understanding. The bell now rings a second time. I must make haste.

"Ivy, I hope all is well. I normally do not have to ring twice."

"I'm sorry Ma'am. Your tarts were coming out of the oven."

"Ivy, sit for a moment, please." I suspect that whatever Mrs. Livingston wishes to say, it is something serious. Normally, she says things directly and then I return to my work. But today she has a few papers on her lap and her brows are furrowed; her tone is somber but direct.

"The Aldridge House is quite a respectable place I've come to understand. I'm sorry, let me begin again. I have made several inquiries into establishments that house orphaned children and provide them with a clean environment and proper education. The Aldridge House comes highly recommended; they have a suitable staff, an orderly shelter, and offer assistance for placements and references when the child comes of age."

I swallow hard. "Ma'am." I take the papers she is offering me and she continues to explain.

"The Aldridge House is just outside of London near the Leicester road. You would be able to visit your niece when you have your holiday by taking the train to the Luton area. The child will have girls her own age to play with... Did I mention it is a school for girls? It is operated by the civil authorities so there are regulations that they must follow, and she will learn a skill. There are no fees for you. She will be cared for." My mistress now grows quiet, perhaps waiting for me to respond. When I do not reply she adds, "You may have tomorrow morning free to take the child and observe it in advance if you'd like. Then, I expect... The Aldridge House has agreed to take the child in two weeks' time."

I still have no idea what I am to say, so I nod my head and simply say, "Yes, Ma'am." It has been decided then, Nolly must go, and a suitable place has been found. She will grow up with other children and learn a skill. I thank Mrs. Livingston and leave the room. Back in the kitchen, Nolly has her arms stretched out in the air surrounding the tarts. She is physically guarding them. What pushes its way through my throat is a bubble of bittersweet laughter.

"I guarded them, Auntie. No one ate them," she says. "Can I go outside to play? It is warmer now that we made tarts."

# 39

## *Margaret*

Within minutes after Ivy leaves my study I see the child for the first time. She is outside in the garden area, bundled in a warm coat and scarf, a knitted hat on her head, and in her small hands she is carrying a basket from which she pulls a jam tart and nibbles on it slowly. She is a tiny slip of a girl, so delicate looking with her golden strands of fine curls and pale white skin. Her hands, though miniature and slender, seemed determined to carry out various tasks. She begins by setting her basket down upon bench nearest the tree, then patiently, one at a time, she carries the empty pots that once held lovely, red geraniums and arranges them in a semi-circle around the bench. She looks around for other objects and finds a discarded carton which she turns over and uses as a table in the center of her play area. She sets the basket down on the carton and then sits inside her little world carrying on conversations with the unseen. She is precious, very precious, indeed. Ivy has cared for her quite well in these past few months, it seems. The child will do quite well at The Aldridge House. She is just the type of adaptable child that can thrive in a place like that. She will be much happier than she is here, all alone, and talking to no one with such animated vigor. Of course, it is best if she leaves before the holiday season begins. Children should be in a lively place during the Christmas season. This old, oversized house filled with priceless antiques is no place for a child. I am no longer convinced that this is the place for me, either. I felt much more relaxed at Grange. It is as if the city harbors grandiose expectations of its residents to continue to be active – a prerequisite to live among the living. Perhaps Mary is right after all; why do I need two large houses? I have no family... Perhaps I should give Mary her due, offer her this house and take myself off to live at our home at Grange-Over-Sands permanently. Ivy can accompany me. It will be less of a strain on her as well. My daily walks along the bay are beneficial and nourishing. The slower pace of life has a much-needed calming effect, and the multiple gardens are a sight for weary eyes. I see with a tug at my heart that the child outside my window has created a safe refuge with just a few old pots and a carton. She seems to instinctively know exactly what she needs and does not burden herself with anything more. It would be quite nice if I could do the same. I need to take very little with me from this house. If I could live without all these encumbrances for half a year, I can live without them forever. This child is a model; she requires little to be quite at peace. The move would be quite simple. I can even leave all the memories of loss behind me. My Chestnut Hill life should tidy up rather nicely. *Because solitude sometimes is the best company, and a brief exile makes sweet return.* Or something to that effect. Wasn't it John Milton who wrote that?

*Don't give up on happiness. Do not remain closed.* Aunt Bess had advised me. If living in this house is the cause of my isolation, then I must leave this house. I do not stroll among the streets of London as I do the promenade at Grange. I do not inhale the fragrance of the sea in this locale, nor do I drink in the visual beauty of the gardens for fear I will encounter someone I know. I slither into the park at night to distract my mind for a few hours but avoid sociability at all costs. In this place I have stopped living, and have been quite content to do so. There is no urgency to decide anything until the spring, however, the dormancy of winter will provide for my need for rest and obscurity. I can remain sheltered for now. All is well.

# 40

## *Old Befana*

What has become evident since leaving my life in my Italian homeland is that this God I've grown so fond of doesn't march through the fields of our lives like a giant in some fairy tale who coddles his favorite creatures and stomps his big feet on the rest. Nor does he sit on the clouds pulling on our puppet strings for his own amusement. This caring God that I found out about from the travelers one night has a way of showing himself that is more obvious than any giant I've ever imagined. He is much larger than anything you can stuff into a single idea of massiveness and the best way to see him is to let him use your eyes. He is easy to recognize in something we call beauty, I daresay. Back home when a magnificent sky is diminished by unrestrained fields of sunflowers you suddenly become aware of the wonder of such a God. Trust me, I'm an old, old Befana. I've been wandering around long enough to know that if there is an indifferent person in charge of things, you won't find beauty like that, much less have an appreciation for it. You could yearn for all eternity for just a taste of beauty but it isn't until you feel the warm strokes of the goodness behind it that you know you are an important part of this vast masterpiece designed by a caring God. What can we offer or add to such grandeur other than our love and appreciation? I get pretty excited when I see how passionate he is about beauty – all *kinds* of beauty. Indifference doesn't give a fig for such things. Even in our darkest moments in life we can still spot magnificence even if only through the eyes of envy. Those who have been slinking around lately spewing crazy remarks about the absence of a caring God have yet to demonstrate any proof to me that nothing at all can have the imagination or capacity to bring about something like a vineyards, poppies and cypress trees scaling the sides of rolling hills. Pah, worms are eating their mothers.

It was in a glorious place called Macerata that I found Benni. He was one of thirteen children and he was smack in the middle of six older brothers, and six younger sisters. To say that he was lost in the rabble is an understatement. With the overabundance of activity in the Torino family it is a wonder that Benni stood out at all, but he most definitely stood out - for the simple reason that Benni was happier than all of his siblings put together. While one brother or another yelled about injustices, or two sisters squabbled over one pair of stockings, or three brothers wrangled over absolutely nothing, Benni wormed his way onto his mother's lap and gave her a kiss. He'd fall in step with his father in the fields and help him hold the yoke of the ox, all while smiling with his mouth wide open. Why Benni even ran to the window first thing in the morning to clap his hands at the rising sun; he'd been known to mimic the rain by jumping up and down like a splashing drop of water. Benni found excitement in the world around him, in things that everyone else was too busy to see. It was Benni's prayers that touched me the most. He would fold his hands tightly together and squeeze his eyes shut and say two simple words: *thank you.* Benni did not have a wide vocabulary; as a matter of fact, he could only speak about ten words all together but those were two of them. He was generally overlooked by his brood of siblings as an anomaly in the family because he was short of stature and had facial features that did not resemble anyone else in the family. Some of the children looked more like their mother with dark hair and eyes and olive skin tones, while some had the more northern complexion of their father with fairer skin and hair. But Benni looked like no one else in the village; he simply looked like Benni.

When Benni was born the midwife told his parents that they should expose him; he wouldn't be much use to them and he wouldn't have long on this earth. But Francesco and Cecilia Torino already had six sons, they weren't looking for usefulness. They refused to expose the infant and were scorned by some people in the village, but they did not care. They loved Benni like the rest of their children. In many ways he was easier to love, for his expectations were simple and his mischief was practically non-existent. He spent his days aiming to please. He would pick flowers from the field and take them to the elderly ladies in town. On cold winter days he would take them small loaves of bread for their supper. In time all of Macerata grew to love little Benni. When he ran outside in the middle of the square clapping his hands at the brilliant sun, the people passing by would join him in clapping their hands. When he waved his arms to and fro to mimic the wind, the people would wave their arms at Benni. When he smiled at them, they always smiled back and greeted him. They only drew the line at jumping up and down like rain drops. He was the town treasure. When I was at Benni's side I followed his appreciation for beauty. What the little guy didn't consciously understand was the beauty that he was. Beauty doesn't have to know it is beautiful to be beauty. The fact that his body and mind put limitations on his ability to learn said nothing about his spirit's ability to grow and shine. He was a poppy that had sprung up in a field of sunflowers and no less delightful for it.

In one sense the midwife had been right, he did not have long on this earth. Even in those final moments he kissed his mother's cheeks and held his father's hand. The villagers that came to visit were greeted with a generous smile. They patted his head and returned the smile through glistening eyes. He had changed something inside each one of them. When his noble heart weakened, it did not take long for him to go very gently in his mother's arms. Still smiling, he closed his eyes and folded his small hands; Benni's final words were *thank you.*

# 41

## *Ivy*

Nolly is beside herself with glee at taking a train ride with me even if it is only as far as Luton. I have only told her that we are going to visit a school, one of many that teach nice little girls. I have not given her a reason except to say that she is getting older now; she will be five years-old soon and five year-old girls begin going to school. I have not mentioned the live-in arrangements. When she questioned me endlessly about why little girls must go to school, why is the school a train ride away, what do little girls wear when they go to school, where are the little boys, when will she start school, and so on, I simply replied with the best answer I could give her: "You know, Nolly, how much you love books and how you pretend to read them and take them with you wherever you go? Well, school will be the place where you really learn how to read those books and you can read them all the time." Her eyes sparkled with such delight that, thankfully, no further answers were required.

After she'd been quiet for a moment she said out loud, "Has your mistress given permission for me to borrow her books yet!"

"No, not yet, my sweet," I replied. "But at school you may ask permission from your teachers to use the school's books." She seemed mollified by the notion of having books and learning to read them. She's been lonely in that big old house. Perhaps Mrs. Livingston was right about sending Nolly away.

In many ways it will certainly make life easier for me and trying to keep up with my household duties. I simply haven't been an adequate guardian for poor Nolly. I have felt quite torn about that. This will be the best solution, most especially for Nolly.

The train depot is but a short walk to the gates of this Elizabethan structure. The outside of Aldridge House does not look like much in the way of academe. The exterior is pleasant enough with a border of holly all along the perimeter of the grounds whose berries are just beginning to flourish. There is a large trellis on the property to the right of the building which covers a few round tables. The chairs are overturned and stacked neatly on top of the tables. Nolly tugs at my sleeve. "Will I be able to play there?" she asks.

"I don't know, love; not without permission from your teachers. There are rules here, too, just like at home." Nolly frowned. Children thrive with the proper dose of rules, though their youth prevents them from understanding this and they see them only as obstacles to their desires.

When we are admitted into the large front doors by the house matron who introduces herself as Miss Withers, Nolly's eyes widen. Aldridge House appears even larger on the inside than it did from the exterior. She will perhaps feel right at home in a place that is large now that she has grown accustomed to the house on Chestnut Hill. Nolly squeezes my hand tightly as we are guided through the dining hall where there are five large tables forming a U-shape facing a long separate table where we're told the food is served buffet style. Mrs. Withers glowers when Nolly interrupts to ask what a buffet style is. Nolly is directing the question to me and I quickly explain that the food is kept separate from the place where people eat; it is not in the center of the dining table. The child is happy to have her question answered but has not missed the disapproval shown by the house matron. She does not ask any more questions until we leave the premises. We are next shown to the kitchen which makes Nolly smile because it looks very similar to the one where she spends a great deal of time with me. Mrs. Withers tells us that teams of children take turns doing various duties: kitchen duties one week, dusting duties the next, washing the next, and so on. Nolly is familiar with chores so this feature of the school presents no problem to her. The dormitory looks quite inviting as well. There are five rooms with ten beds in each room and all the beds are neatly covered with patchwork quilts donated by benefactors of the school. I cannot read Nolly's reaction to the dormitory, she looks neither pleased, nor concerned.

Finally, we view the two classrooms through large windows. One classroom is for older girls and they are learning some of the complexities of mathematics. The other room is for the younger girls who are learning the fundamentals of reading. Between the two classrooms is what Mrs. Withers calls the workshop where girls are taught various skills such as sewing, knitting, typing, transcribing, and so on...

Nolly has quietly taken in the narrative that accompanies the tour. Mrs. Withers explained by rote the hours of school, the schedule for study time, chores, eating, sleeping, reading and skill training. There was no mention of play time. This will be Nolly's first step toward structured living. As she takes it all in there are particles of wonder forming around the corners of her eyes which at some point may gather together and form into fear. To me, these cloistered children resemble little animals taken from the wild and tempered to live in a carefully constructed menagerie; each one of them has sought their own kind. It is difficult for me to discern whether it is Nolly's present loneliness or her future assimilation that will do more to inhibit her free spirit.

As the tour nears its completion Mrs. Withers explains the holiday schedule, visiting regulations, and such information that governs their policies in the event of illness. Nolly is now sitting by the window looking at a cat that is prowling about just outside in the garden while I ask several more questions and receive the application forms that I will need to complete and send in before the child arrives. Are there any special circumstances that the school should be made aware of? Any chronic illnesses? Any unusual patterns of behavior? These matters must be disclosed up front before an application will be considered. I assure Mrs. Withers that Nolly is a healthy, well-adjusted child and that she has proven to be quite adaptable. Mrs. Withers forms what might pass as a smile but looks more like a smirk as if she has heard these words a thousand times before. She escorts us back to the front of the house with such strictness that I wonder if she thinks I will simply abandon Nolly at this very moment and disappear without a trace.

Before we depart from Aldridge House the girls have completed their morning lessons and walk quietly past the front hall toward the large parlor where they are encouraged to have quiet time. I look carefully into their eyes, looking for clues as to how they feel about living here. They have a look I recognize from a time long ago. These children may have nothing to call their own except for one thing, they possess an unspoken hope as I once did. Their sentences begin with "when." *When I grow up, I will... When I get out of this place, I will... When I find the right person, I will...*

At what point, I wonder, does the word "when" change to "why?" *Why did I ever make this decision or that?... Why did I not listen to my parents? Why am I in this situation?* Nolly looks up at my face and squeezes my hand more tightly. I remind her to thank Mrs. Withers for the tour and she whispers a thank you and waves good-bye, tugging me toward the door.

For the hour that we must wait for the train to return home Nolly leans her head against my arm as we sit uncomfortably on the narrow cement seating that adjoins the pale yellow wall with the plastered train schedule. I ask her what she thinks of Aldridge House. She answers simply, "When I come home on holidays I can sleep with you in your bedchamber again?"

# 42

## *Margaret*

Upon their return from a visit to Aldridge House Ivy and her niece seemed quite placated. I trust the visit went well. I watched as they came up the walk and noticed that the child was jovially pointing to the garden area in a pleading manner. Ivy accompanies her to the bench sits down. The child leisurely climbs onto Ivy's lap and Ivy rocks the child and speaks to her for several minutes until they both break out in laughter. Odd, they both share a mannerism of holding their stomachs when they laugh. I don't know that I've ever seen Ivy laugh before. This tender moment between them ends when the child jumps off Ivy's lap and begins to play. Ivy seems to give her instructions before she circles the house to enter through the servant's door by the kitchen.

Once again the child is arranging the flower pots and carton as she had before, for she had meticulously put everything away after she was finished playing the last time. What is it with this child and her urge to create nests? This time she removes something small from her coat pocket and sets it on the carton table in the center of her domain. She is speaking to the object in a very spirited way using her arms to gesticulate a different movement for each sentence. Suddenly I notice that the child is speaking to an object that does not belong to her. I quickly glance toward the shelf near my desk and notice that my figurine of the old woman is missing! The child has removed my statuette. She must have taken it when they went out to Aldridge House this morning. I watch the child as she sits near the carton and now grows quiet with her head propped in her hands, staring intently at the statue and nodding her head. She can't possibly think she is *listening*? I pace the room wondering how to approach this matter with Ivy. This is just a small child and I trust she means no harm but certainly this behavior cannot be encouraged for her own sake!

I wait a few moments for Ivy to catch her breath and change back into her service apron. I ring the bell and when she appears I ask if all went well with their visit to Aldridge House to which she merely responds, "Yes, Ma'am."

"It has occurred to me, Ivy, that I have yet to meet your niece. I should like to do so before she departs for school. Would you ask her to please come in to my study for a few moments? Perhaps you can bring us a little tea and some of those tarts you made the other day."

"Yes, Ma'am." Ivy backs out of the room slowly with a hint of suspicion in her eyes. Well, of course she is suspicious. She is fully aware that I have not spoken to children in quite some time. I fear that Ivy would suffer an attack of panic if I told her why I need to speak to the child so it's best if I do it discreetly. If she is as protective of that child as she is of me, she must surely be in a state of flux these days. Poor Ivy, I wish social conventions did not keep us at arms' length from one another. There are many times when I feel like there is an unspoken sisterhood between us, much stronger than that which I share with my own sisters. In this house all I can do is treat her as a servant.

After several minutes Ivy escorts the child into the study and I invite the child to sit down on the low Jacobean armchair across from my own. Ivy sets the tray of tea and tarts between us. The child wiggles backward into the chair until her feet stretch out directly in front of her. I ask Ivy if she would be so kind as to run down to the chemist for some kola concoction, explaining that I feel a headache coming on. Nervously, Ivy leaves me alone with the child.

Good heavens, at that moment I realize that I have never even asked Ivy the child's name. It seems reasonable to begin there. The child looks up at me with the most intense violet eyes I have ever seen. She is very dear, I can see. She bears no resemblance to Ivy who has darker features but there is something quite familiar about her in the way she waits for a cue. She seems quite calm while I feel rather unsteady in my mission.

"May I ask your name? We haven't been properly introduced," I begin.

She straightens her back and sits upright. "My name is Nollaig Brigid Doyle. But Auntie calls me Nolly for short. May I ask your name?"

How direct she is! I pause before answering. She is not what I expected. I'm not quite certain what I expected but she does not whimper or snivel like some children might. She seems rather confident and older than her four years of age. "My name is Margaret Katherine Livingston," I reply. "But most people call me Mrs. Livingston." She continues to look at me, waiting for another cue. "Your name is quite lovely, very Irish," I tell her. It's not a question so she does not respond. This child intrigues me.

"Your Auntie Ivy tells me that you went to visit a school today. Did you like the school?"

She puts her finger on her chin as if she must consider the proper response and then she says, "Auntie says the school is suitable. There was a garden outside. I should like to spend time in the garden."

"You like gardens, Nolly?"

"Yes, I do. I like them very much. It's because of the sprouts."

"The sprouts?"

She nods. "Mommy showed me how to put something in the ground and then it sprouts. Nothing sprouts inside a house or anywhere else, really, except in a garden. Things sprout."

"You are very clever, Nolly." There is the slightest suggestion of a smile forming at the corners of her lips. "Your Ivy... your auntie brought us some tea and some tarts. May I pour you some tea?"

"Yes, thank you, Mrs. Livyst..." She cups her hand over her mouth. Now I cannot help but smile.

"You're right, Mrs. Livingston is a mouthful. You can shorten it to Missus if you'd like."

"Thank you Missus. I helped my auntie make the tarts. I pressed the dough and spooned the jam."

As we drank our tea, I broached the nature of my mission quite carefully. "Nolly, I saw you playing outside in my garden. Do you like the garden? Is anything sprouting?

"No, Missus. It is almost winter. Nothing will sprout in the winter. It is a time of rest."

"This is true. Things seem to be resting out there. But, you seem to be quite fond of forming a little refuge, an enclosed area in which to play. Do you feel safe in the smaller play area?" Nolly furrowed her brows and seemed perplexed by my question. I try to clarify. "Why do you build little places to play?"

"Oh," she replied, "they're not for me, but it's a secret, Missus. I must make a comfortable place so I put things around to make it more like a little house."

"Do you have visitors?"

She stares at me directly and I can see the reluctance to respond to any more questions building a little fence between us. She is not certain of my motives. "I'm sorry, I don't mean to pry. I'm just curious."

She tilts her head to the right and looks at me carefully before answering. "Yes, Missus. I do, but it's a secret. Will you promise not to tell?"

"I promise," I answer.

"After you went to the sea, my Mommy went to heaven."

"I know, Nolly. I am terribly sorry. Your Auntie Ivy told me. I'm sorry."

"But before she went to heaven, Mommy said that heaven isn't a faraway place like Ireland. Whenever I need Mommy I just have to make a soft place for her and she will be here and we can be together. She isn't far away at all. She promised to stay close by." For a moment she grows quiet and then she says. "I feel Mommy with me in the comfy place."

She speaks so plainly and with such confidence, I am at a loss for words. More than that, I feel my well-guarded reserve crumbling beneath me so I suddenly do not wish to continue.

"I see. Well, I suppose it is time for you to return to your auntie. She must be back from the chemist's by now. You may leave the tea cup here on the tray and take an extra tart with you. It was very nice to meet you Nolly."

"It was nice to meet you, too, Missus." On the way out, Nolly pauses by the shelf near my desk and sets my figurine in its rightful place. I had completely forgotten to ask her about it, so rattled did I become at the direction our conversation had taken. The child seems unfazed by the fact that I ended our discourse so abruptly particularly after she had just shared a personal and sentimental secret. She closes the door behind her and for the next hour or two I pace the room back and forth, reminding myself that she will leave in just two weeks and that I will turn this house over to Mary in just a few months; I can move back to Grange and I needn't be bothered with such unsettling conversations again. I'm sorry I sent her away like that. She is very dear.

# 43

## *Old Befana*

No one wants to be without a family. I don't remember ever being part of one in my younger days; at times I would feel like something was missing even if I did not know what it was. I've found that people will do anything, sometimes the wrong things, just to feel like they are a part of something that holds them together. Love, acceptance, power, rationales – these can get all mixed up and soon you can't distinguish one from the other. But one thing remains clear, people form families no matter what they have to do and those that flee from them simply feel like their efforts have failed and it's too painful to try again.

Some families look funny – I mean really *funny*. And not too long ago I was part of one such family. This happened to be a family of objects – that's right - we were similar in purpose but quite distinct in appearance and nature. We sat on top of a very long mantel that extended the length of one wall over a sturdy stone fireplace bulging with granite and limestone rocks of all shapes and sizes. It was quite a cozy place; we rarely moved from this spot, but from the mantel we could see the room where we'd all come together. It was neat and clean; it had one sofa and several overstuffed chairs but everything was covered in homemade, very colorful afghans. The colors varied in each square but all the squares were framed in black and it gave the room a very warm feeling. There was a window across from us and all we could see, day and night, month after month, was snow. The woman that lived in this snug little cottage was old, *really old*. Like me – well, maybe not that old but she always wore the same black dress and a crocheted shawl around her shoulders. She sat in her cottage day after day crocheting something new from the bales of yarn next to her favorite chair by the window. Every now and then she would get up and come over to the mantel and dust off the family.

I think there were about ten or fifteen of us up there. We never got to change places; we had assigned spots. The only time we moved was when the children came over to visit, probably grandchildren. They were allowed to take us down to visit with us. They knew all of our names – every one of us!

There was Stekkjastaur, he was from Iceland. He had peg-legs and he was usually the one the children laughed at the most until they banished him to the corner of the room for not bringing enough presents at Christmas. He was one of thirteen yule-lads but the old woman had not yet collected the whole set. He had a friend named Gluggagaegir and another named Ketkrokur. Together, along with the rest of their friends, they were known as tricksters. For some reason they were fond of playing pranks on people but particularly around the Christmas season. They were an amusing bunch of lads. They did not know how to be serious. Eventually, they were all banished to the corner of the room while the children were playing with the rest of us.

Then there was Tomte from Scandinavia. He looked elf-like really but a skinny elf at that. He wasn't as prankish as the yule-lads but he had quite the sense of humor; you could tell by his rascally grin. Dressed a lot like a woodsman, he seemed quite out of place in the festive little sleigh that he sat on. No one could see what was in the bags stuffed into his sleigh but the way he kept his eye on them, it had to be something good!

A character that looked a lot like Tomte was Belsnickel who one minute said he was from somewhere in Germany and the next minute he swore he was from Austria. I don't think he really knew where he was from. I'd never heard of him before but this guy did not smile much. He was pretty fierce looking all dressed up in furs and looking like he was from a clan of cave bears. It was his job to scare children into being good, kind of like his buddy Krampus who was supposed to terrify naughty kids. It seemed to be an act, though. They really loved kids as much as the rest of us. It was only the old woman's grandson that played with them. He'd hold them up and growl at his sister until she either wept or used the Dutch guy Sinterklaas to chase them off.

The few that looked similar to each other were Pere Noel from France, Babo Natale from Italy, and Father Christmas from England. They all seemed to wear the same clothes, sported the same overgrown facial hair, and dressed in red fur (a color that does not come naturally to any furry creature that I'm aware of!) But these guys were the nice guys. It was their job to bring presents to nice children on Christmas morning. They always smiled and they even developed a trademark laugh to distinguish them from everyone else.

This family had a few females, too, fear not! I was one of them. My legend keeps me searching for children in case I should find the Christ child so I leave gifts for all of them; I don't mess around with naughty or nice. Eerily, I also discovered I have a twin in Russia named Baboushka. We look a lot alike and our stories sound much the same, but I think I've kept my figure a little bit better than she has.

Ded Moroz has a granddaughter named Snegurochka, and they come from eastern Europe. The old guy, Ded, used to be a mean fella but now he brings gifts to children to make up for his sordid past, and his granddaughter, the snow maiden, helps him stay on track.

I can't forget Ông già Noel – he's from Vietnam. Oh, he's a character! The guy loves parties and he knows how to rile up the lot of us in fun and fellowship. I always liked Ông.

Together, the bunch of us, we're on a mission of giving and we do get around the world one way or another. You know what I think about this whole business of giving presents at Christmas time? I think it's all part of a bigger plan. It's no secret. We're not really living unless we're giving. This strange little family I belong to, that's our job. We all, not just this family, but *everyone* has something special to give and that's what keeps us going. Giving means you fill something so it doesn't have to ever feel empty or afraid, whether it's the mind, the heart, the stomach, or a void. We're meant to give what we have out of love. That's the great big plan. When we stop giving, we stop living. It is this spirit of giving that has kept us alive. We are ambassadors of joy.

## 44

*Ivy*

How is it possible for something so reasonable to feel so unreasonable? In trying to encourage Nolly get used to the idea that she must go away and live at Aldridge House I feel like it is I who must get used to the idea. Has my life been more difficult since she came here? Yes. Would it be easier for me to do my job if I did not have to worry about her? Yes. Have I felt less lonely in my life since she came to stay? Yes. Has my life had more meaning and fulfillment since she came? Absolutely.

I know Mrs. Livingston is right; I've seen it with my own eyes, Aldridge House will be the best place for Nolly. I simply cannot offer her the attention, the education, the opportunities, and the care that a community can offer her. Nolly does not seem upset about leaving, which is a sign I believe that she knows this is best, too. Perhaps she welcomes the idea of being in a place that can offer her so much more than I can. Selfishly, I suppose, I want her to prefer to stay with me than to adapt so well to the idea of leaving, but then I would have to work harder to convince her to go and I'm not sure I can.

Today she has insisted that I ask the Missus for permission to play with some of the books in the study. She wants to *read* them, she says. And she wants permission to read them to granny. I've been reluctant to ask so I keep telling Nolly that the Missus is too busy right now to be disturbed, or the

Missus seems to be in a distressed mood so maybe now is not the time. The latter is closer to the truth. I don't know what transpired between Nolly and my mistress on the day we returned from Aldridge House but Mrs. Livingston seems quite agitated. I have asked Nolly if the conversation went well and she smiles brightly and tells me they had tea and tarts and they talked about gardens. When I asked Mrs. Livingston if my niece was polite during their visit she looked at me intently and responded, "Of course she was. It was an enlightening visit." That was all she said. What could have been so enlightening about gardens? Well, knowing Nolly as I do, anything could have come out of that child's mouth.

"Ivy, is there something on your mind? You've dusted those shelves several times now," Mrs. Livingston says.

"Well, yes Ma'am, there is. It's Nolly. She has asked me to ask your permission to borrow a book or two... and to borrow the figurine of the old woman. She wishes to pretend to read to her. She calls it granny."

"Ah, I see. She has played with it before then?"

Oh, dear. I might as well dust off the layers of deception in this room as well. "Yes, Ma'am. I am sorry. Nolly is quite taken with that figurine. None other. She seems to feel that it represents something she does not have – a grandmother. She pretends to read to her or to invite her to her little imaginative encounters. She is quite gentle. I do apologize for her assertiveness in borrowing it without permission in the past. It was my responsibility to watch her more closely." I can't help it, at that moment all the anxiety about sending Nolly away catches up with me. I do something I can't seem to stop myself from doing lately. I begin to cry.

Again, Mrs. Livingston seems to recoil from my emotional display. She's not used to it either. She walks over to the window and stares outside for several long moments, giving me a chance to compose myself. Finally, she turns around and says in a gentle voice, "Nolly may borrow a book or two and she may read them to "granny" but she must not take them out of the study. You may bring her in here while you clean. I will be upstairs for the afternoon; I have some sorting to do. I do not wish to be disturbed."

"Yes, Ma'am. Thank you. I'm sorry I..." but Mrs. Livingston leaves the room before I can finish my apology for my emotional state. Nolly must have been lurking near the door and heard the whole discussion. She was probably trying to make sure I asked what she wanted me to ask. I hear Mrs. Livingston say excuse me as she leaves the study. Nolly walks in quietly and finds me on the sofa still sobbing silently. She puts both of her tiny arms around my shoulders and lays her head against my cheek. I pull her closer to me and we remain like that for a long time, neither of us saying a word.

After quite some time, Nolly goes over to the books and with both arms carries a rather unused copy of Dickens' Nicholas Nickleby. She sets the book down on the sofa and then brings granny over as well so that they can huddle together next to me. Nolly opens the large book to a random page and tells me to read. I take a deep breath and begin. "When I speak of home, I speak of the place where in default of a better--those I love are gathered together; and if that place were a gypsy's tent, or a barn, I should call it by the same good name notwithstanding."

I kiss the top of Nolly's head. I think I now know what I must do.

# 45

## *Margaret*

I have only filled one carton with personal belongings and perhaps it is sufficient. The heirlooms in this house, those in the attic, those in all its bedchambers, the parlor, the music room – everything – should probably go to Mary and she can do with them what she will. What will I do with all of this when it should come my time to go? She can divide it between herself and Anne, if my youngest sister is interested in anything at all. Mary is able to bequeath all of this to her children. I simply want to gather my own personal effects during the coming winter for what there is in the house at Grange is also more than adequate for one person. It is simply a matter of emotional detachment at this point and I find it difficult to believe that my life on Chestnut Hill is winding down. It is a relief in one sense, but it is also a source of regret. So much loss.

The carton that was already packed was filled with mementos that I'd put away after David's departure nearly two years ago. A few photos, some old letters, and quite a few keepsakes that are best hidden away. I still cannot bear to look at them. Perhaps I never shall. So why keep them, I wonder? The souvenirs of love are not a substitute for love itself; they are just reminders that you are now living without that integral part in life, yet it is so difficult to part with them. I feel it is impossible.

I try to take courage and open the carton carefully like a squeamish person undressing a wound. Is it possible to only look at the memories that soothe and avoid the ones that will chafe? Memories are generally taken as a whole, just like life itself, the good along with the bad, or the *really bad*. There are ribbons tied carefully around tissue paper that enfold a few portraits of David and I, when we became engaged and when we were married. Untying the ribbons is a major step for me; I have not wanted to see him, talk to him, or listen to him because our dreams ended so badly and I know that I am just as responsible as he is. These pictures, particularly the one of us on our wedding day in front of this house, in such a perfect embrace, the type where souls are locked together through an inexpressible bond of love, is the most haunting. At our gallant reception here that followed the wedding, David had read my favorite of Shelley's poems,

*The fountains mingle with the river*
*And the rivers with the ocean,*
*The winds of heaven mix for ever*
*With a sweet emotion;*
*Nothing in the world is single;*
*All things by a law divine*
*In one spirit meet and mingle.*
*Why not I with thine? —*
*See the mountains kiss high heaven*
*And the waves clasp one another;*
*No sister-flower would be forgiven*
*If it disdained its brother;*
*And the sunlight clasps the earth*
*And the moonbeams kiss the sea:*
*What is all this sweet work worth*
*If thou kiss not me?*

David was a romantic. He believed that love was meant to be something enduring and that it was responsible only for joy.

185

He could not prevail through love's trials, those moments when joy had vanished. The society column that announced our matrimony stated, "*If ever two people were destined for happiness, David and Margaret Livingston.*" From that day to this, what happened – from lovers joined in heart and spirit to individuals as far removed as east is from west. Only a few short years later the same column followed up with a social commentary, "*What God has joined together, a tragedy can put asunder.*" Our heartbreak had been splashed across the papers for the judgment and pastime of others; all of it, illness, death and disillusionment. My deepest fears were made public. Shouldn't our fears be a private matter? Without looking any further into the carton I put everything back inside; I've seen enough for today.

# 46

## *Old Befana*

If I've given the impression that I'm a tough old woman who is rattled by nothing, I should clarify; I get ruffled by storms. Windstorms, thunderstorms and blizzards aren't very pleasant for an elderly woman who gets around with a broom and a sack on her back. As far as I'm concerned when you are using a star as your compass any storm can be dangerous if you lose sight of the focal point; that's why you need your internal compass because when you get to be my age, or any age for that matter, you need to know the direction that will keep you steady; you need to remember your where your heart is. Storms give me the jitters; they can happen with the weather, but they can also happen with people, and let me tell you a storm is brewing around here and I'm not very confident about how it will end, and I just hate it when storms are so bad they make everything break apart. Some things can be restored, some things cannot. Human hearts can only take so much. Ivy knows this. Margaret knows this, too. It's the child I'm worried about.

Margaret's decisions about the changes in her life and the lives of others seem to be final, but is she at peace with them? Something locked away in the belly of her worst fears seems eager to be released. In her brave, aristocratic way she is struggling to keep the hatch closed on the turbulence but the calm she hopes for is brewing up into a squall.

Ivy has discovered the devastating tug between love and duty like the soldier who must weigh security against sacrifice. She hasn't slept soundly since Margaret's return and her nerves are quite frayed. The room seems airless when Ivy walks into the study.

"I never wish to sound ungrateful, Ma'am," Ivy begins, "because I will be indebted to your kind charity for the rest of my life. Your family gave me a home and a means to make a living, and when my sister and her child were in need you allowed them to come into your home as well. Your generosity means so much to me."

"Generosity?" Margaret unexpectedly slams down the piano cover. She'd never raised her voice in Ivy's presence and Ivy trembles with alarm. Margaret takes a moment to lower the volume of her voice but the tone becomes even and harsh. "It was not generosity to hire you in service at a pittance, Ivy. And what did it cost me to let your family come here in their time of need? Tell me, what did it cost *me*? Nothing. Generosity without some sort of sacrifice is of little value. We can console ourselves that we've done a good deed by others but if we remain untouched by it we are fooling ourselves. We give a great deal of lip service to generosity but there was no charity involved. How can it be called charity if it cost me nothing personally? If we are spared the pang of love because we give from excess in one form or another can we really consider ourselves charitable? I wasn't even here when your sister was ill and died. I could have been more help to you if I had been, if I could just stop thinking of all that has transpired in this house. But, no, I had the opportunity to escape, to go to another home, to avoid facing my losses. Do not judge my actions to be generous or charitable when you simply benefitted from my cowardice!"

This all began because Ivy dropped the tray she was carrying and the mistress' favorite tea service shattered on the marble floors. It was an antique that her own grandmother had cherished. Ivy had tripped over one of Nolly's little nests and the tray went flying out of her hands. Ivy knelt down and in tears began picking up the pieces. Nolly knelt next to her and tried to help but Ivy had pushed her away and began scolding her for the mess and for touching the broken pieces because she might get hurt. Ivy sobbed and Nolly put her fist in own small mouth to keep from sobbing even more than her auntie. Margaret had been quietly reading in the study when she heard the commotion and came quickly into the hall to find Ivy reprimanding Nolly. She assessed the situation quickly and bent down to take Nolly by the hand. She assured Ivy that the tea set would be one less thing for Mary to enjoy but Ivy did not hear or understand its meaning. Margaret led Nolly into the music room which was located on the other side of the study. Nolly had never been able to venture into this room; the door handle was much too high and the door was always closed.

When Margaret and Nolly entered the room the mishap was quickly forgotten. Nolly dropped her fist from her mouth and stared up at the Missus with eyes wide of wonderment.

"This is the music room, Nolly. Do you enjoy music?" Nolly did not respond with words but her eyes lit up with anticipation. "I haven't been in this room myself in a very long time. I used to play this piano every day, but now I've put all such things away. Would you like me to play you a small melody?" Nolly nodded her head. "Come sit beside me on the bench and let us see if I can recall how to play."

Margaret began to play an old tune called *Dainty Davie* and Nolly wiggled her fingers in the air imitating the Missus and clapping her hands after the song ended. Suddenly, Margaret's heart felt unusually light and she'd nearly forgotten her typical frame of mind. When Margaret began to play again Nolly hopped off the bench and began to dance alongside the piano. Margaret could not help but smile. When she finished the tune, Nolly exclaimed, "You are very good, Missus. The piano is always sleeping but when you touch it, it wakes up happy!"

Just then, Ivy walked into the room and told Nolly that her lunch was waiting for her in the kitchen. Nolly thanked the Missus for playing the piano and walked out quietly past Ivy, afraid that she was still in trouble. Ivy closed the door and walked over toward Margaret.

"Ma'am, I am so very sorry about breaking the tea service. You can take my wages for it," she said.

"Nonsense, Ivy. Honestly, you've nothing to apologize for; these things happen. Please do not give this another thought."

"You are too kind, Ma'am, and generous. I have been giving this situation a great deal of thought. You were right; this arrangement is difficult on Nolly, where she can play, what she can touch and not touch, she's young and she doesn't always understand. I have tried, Ma'am, honestly, I have tried, but she needs more than I can give her under these circumstances." Ivy bites her lower lip and pauses for a moment.

"Have you sent in your application for Aldridge House, then?" Margaret asks her.

"No, Ma'am, I have not."

"But, Ivy, I thought you just said you understood the difficulties of this arrangement."

"I do, Ma'am, but I'm thinking of Nolly. You are right; she needs to be around other children. She is nearly old enough to begin school, and she requires a more disciplined environment that still allows her to be a child. But, Ma'am, I cannot send her away. I simply cannot. Is not family an important thing for a child to have as well? She has lost her family; I am all she has. She is not an orphan entirely. We have each other." Ivy remained steadfast in her resolve but tears were quietly rolling down her cheeks. "I will give you sufficient notice, Ma'am. I am trying to find a position which will allow me to work during the day while Nolly is at school and when she comes home in the afternoon, she will have me there and my full attention as well. Please forgive me, Ma'am.

I have been very happy here and I appreciate all that you have done for me. You have been very generous, but I feel that I must go – that Nolly and I must go together."

That was what brought on the storm.

# 47

## *Margaret*

After lunch, I called Ivy back in for a small chat. She has agreed to remain at least until after the Christmas holidays but I believe she is harboring her own disappointment and frustration. She is very quiet now, more so than usual. I suppose there is very little left to say between us. She says she is looking for a position that will allow her more time with the child. I know she is trying to look out for the best interests of her young niece, but I cannot help feeling like I'm about to endure another great loss. Ivy has been at my side through so many difficulties. I was so confident I would be bringing her with me to Grange, but she seems rather adamant about her decision and I feel somewhat hurt that I am about to lose her. At least I have persuaded her to remain through the holidays for the child's sake. It's important for Nolly that Christmas should be spent in familiar surroundings and not in transit to strange locales. For me, the Christmas holidays have been more pain than pleasure so who am I kidding? I claim to want them here for the holidays for their sake, but it is possible I want them here for myself. I need to think things through. I have given Ivy the afternoon off and a bit of money to take Nolly to enjoy the day at the carousel before it closes for the winter. I need time alone.

*God, if you can still hear me I just want you to know how angry I feel.* Without warning the plate in front of me with the uneaten fruit goes flying out of my hand and smashes against the wall. I seem to be unable to stop throwing everything within my reach. *God! Hear me! Listen to me! I have no one, there is no one to whom I can express how broken I feel, how terrified I am, how, how...* When no further words are available I simple scream. And shout. *I beg you. Weren't those my final words to you, God? I beg you. Tell me, now what am I supposed to do? What can I do when peace is nowhere to be found? I'm alone and I don't know what to do.*

\*\*\*

Following my tirade and Ivy's return, I sense that there is an unmistakable tension in the air; all of us seem on edge these days. Quietly, like nannies tiptoeing around a sleeping child, we perform daily duties. Ivy is still caring for this home, the child, and myself; Nolly still plays alone in any corner she can find and wiles away the hours with that figurine she's grown attached to; I don't seem to mind that she is so fond of it. She uses some old cushions I have donated to her cause and a wooden carton to create her little hovel. I spend my own time taking care of my business affairs and putting plans into motion to move away from this home, sorting through memorabilia and all that I will leave behind. There are a few keepsakes of my mother's that I should like to take along. It is so much easier to allow things to accumulate, to find a nook in which to store them rather than to make *decisions* about them. Sorting through one's past takes an emotional toll. The sooner I accomplish this, the better. No more Christmases in this house. No more memories.

I watch as Nolly brings a small broken twig from the fir tree at the side of the house. She is arranging it in her box in the hall as a Christmas tree. For decorations she is tying a few of her hair ribbons on its branches and then puts the old woman statue close by. I step into the hall as she finishes her ministrations.

"Nolly," I call her.

"Yes, Missus." She hasn't looked up from her box.

"Nolly, can you come into the study for a moment?"

As all children do, she dawdles by completing her game before entering the study. "I'm here, Missus. Do you want tea?"

"That is a wonderful idea. I would love some tea. Please go ask your auntie to bring us all some tea."

Nolly returns carrying the tea towels and Ivy brings in the tray. I ask both of them to sit down. They both choose to sit together closely on the sofa, like they are joined at the hip. Rigidly, Ivy serves the tea. She is not as relaxed as she used to be. They both wait until I have taken a sip of my own tea before they lift their cups to their lips.

"It is nearly Christmas," I begin, "and I should like for the three of us to spend Christmas together." Ivy begins to fidget nervously and looks at me strangely, but I continue. "Everything will change so much after the holidays, you will go to your new home and I will go to Grange, and I just feel that it would be very special if we can use this time to make some final memories." They both sit quietly because they probably don't completely understand what that entails, so I continue. "I should like for us to decorate the house with Christmas ornamentation and to have a special meal together – all three of us in the dining room instead of me taking my meal alone in there. Perhaps a bit of caroling at the piano. It's just that having Nolly here... well, for her sake."

Ivy simply replies, "Yes, Ma'am," as if I have asked her to clean the guest rooms, or bring my tray up to my room but Nolly smiles largely. Ivy finishes her tea and asks to be excused. She tells Nolly to do the same but I intercede. "I would like Nolly's opinion on where the Christmas tree should be erected; she can remain behind for a few moments. I have asked Mr. Styles from the tree lot to deliver a tree tomorrow morning. Ivy, if you can bring the cartons with ornaments from the storage room, I would appreciate it. "Yes, Ma'am," she says, and leaves the room. I sigh. "Fine, well, shall we begin trying to figure out where to put the tree?" I ask Nolly. She hops off the sofa and sets her teacup carefully on the tray. She puts her finger to her chin again as she does when she is pondering a question, then she turns around and asks, "Can we put it by the window? I think we can move the plants."

"I think that is a very good idea," I tell her. "You are clever." She straightens up with pride.

"May I help you decorate it, Missus?"

"Nolly, of course you may help me. I cannot decorate a Christmas tree alone. No one should put up such decorations without any help. Some of the ornaments are very old and very fragile, but you may hang the durable ones within your reach."

"Is it a big tree, Missus?"

"It is big enough, I should think."

"I've seen Christmas trees before, small ones, but Mommy said someday I would have a Christmas tree that is big. Why do people put up Christmas trees, Missus?"

"It brings joy into the home. It reminds us about life and about the gladness we're meant to experience, that the Baby Jesus brought us both life and joy – and hope."

"Do all babies do that?"

"Yes, Nolly, I believe they do, but Baby Jesus brought more than any other baby because he was God's very own baby."

"And the Ayle Mary's." I had to smile at her brogue-ish pronunciation. "Did you ever have a baby, Missus?"

For a moment I am stunned at her question, but in her innocence she does not understand why that is a painful question for me. When will I ever be able to get near the answers to such questions again?

"I did, Nolly. I once had a baby." The child senses my somberness and asks nothing more. I do not wish for her to feel awkward for having asked and I fear what questions she may still ask, so I volunteer the only information I'm prepared to give. "He was a baby boy. His name was Joseph and he lived only a couple of years."

"Joseph, just like the Baby Jesus' Daddy's name," she says. "Mommy told me that Joseph loved the Baby Jesus. God was Baby Jesus' real Daddy in heaven, but Joseph took very good care of him. When a Mommy or a Daddy lives in heaven, God gives the baby new ones."

"Sometimes, Nolly. That's right."

"Your Joseph is with my Mommy?"

With a tightened throat I answer "Yes."

"He still loves you like my Mommy still loves me. Did you make a comfy place for him?" she asks.

"I beg your pardon?" I ask her.

"Mommy told me to make sure I make a comfy place for her where she can stay with me. Did you make a comfy place for Joseph?" I cannot answer. I rise and walk to the window. "Tomorrow we shall move the plants, Nolly, and Mr. Styles will bring the tree." My voice is trembling.

She leaves the room silently, closing the door behind her. *No, Nolly, I have not made a comfy place. Dear Joseph, I am so sorry, I have not made a comfy place for you in my heart. My dear little Joseph…*

# 48

## *Ivy*

For fifteen years I have lived and worked in this home; it is all I have known. I have lived here even longer than I lived with my family in Ireland. I never imagined that I would have to move on from here. In my dreams I could not have imagined that a small child would cause me to want anything else. I have no other skills other than housekeeping and it only for this work I am qualified. Our future is uncertain and I don't know if I'm doing the right thing because I cannot see the future. My decision will ensure a life of struggles and maybe even hardship. "Colleen, what do you want me to do? I love Nolly like she is my own. If you were here to advise me, what would you have me do?" Tears fall on my shaking hands. I've always handled the objects in this home with such care and today I just don't care. I'm slamming things just short of breaking them. I just can't send Nolly away. I fear I am doing this as much for myself as for her. Am I being selfish? Have I reached a point in my life where I would like something other than work to call my own? I do love her; she has brought joy into this home by no other means than just being a child. Just look at Mrs. Livingston – why Nolly seems to have blown a bit of breath on the embers of my mistress' careworn heart. I could have lived here another seventy years and never accomplished that.

My mistress has agreed to look after Nolly for the afternoon while I seek other employment and submit my references which she has graciously provided. I am indebted to Mrs. Livingston, but in my heart I feel quite angry with her for having placed me in this position. It is not her fault. She is right in her recommendation to have Nolly placed in a proper home for girls, but I still feel distressed that everything is changing. I have seen her packing a few boxes. Though she hasn't told me I believe that she will not return once she goes back to Grange after the winter. She has that decisive countenance about her, not the stagnancy of the past two years. For once, she seems to be prepared to take a step in a new direction. I suppose the time has come for all of us to do so.

After several hours of inquiries I have found nothing promising. Shopkeepers have expressed no need for a woman with my skills, nor are they willing to train me to deal in their trades. Offices have no need for unskilled clerks. I know how to clean, and housekeepers keep long hours, not conducive to raising a child. I have walked through this entire sector without so much as a glimmer of hope.

It is bitterly cold today. The wind is assaulting my mood as well as my stamina. I fumble in my pocket for my handkerchief and suddenly finger the little rosary Nolly offered me for "good luck" before I left. On my own I have not prayed the rosary since I lived at home with Ma who made us say it nightly. Nolly has asked me to join her in saying it before she falls asleep at night – of course it is quite an abridged version if there ever was one. This routine of Nolly's says so much about Colleen's ability to carry on the faith with her daughter passed down to us from our parents. I suppose I left the faith behind when I boarded a ferry for England. I had other ambitions. Am I prepared to give Nolly what she needs in this respect as well? Lord, help me. I know she would not have a proper catechism at the Aldridge House. But, what do I know about the faith? As Christmas approaches, I've been telling her the stories, though not without correction. "It was the shepherds who came first, Auntie, not the kings. They came later and brought the presents. The shepherds didn't see a star, they heard angels. The kings didn't hear angels, they saw a star. Different things brought people to the Baby Jesus, Auntie." And then of course, there is the bit that's not in the Bible, "and granny shows children how to find him and believe. That's her job." She says this so matter-of-factly as if she has it on firm authority.

The cold has seeped into my bones and now a light snow is beginning to fall. I find a bench just outside of St. Bedes and sit to rest. I can hear the choir practicing inside. It is just two weeks until Christmas. A soloist launches into a solemn recital of *El Noi de la Mare*. I don't understand a word of this hymn but I don't have to; it is sung with a deep and rich love for God you can feel its determination to worship him. It is much warmer inside the church. Perhaps I can step in just for a moment to listen to this hymn.

*Què li darem a n'el Noi de la Mare?*
*Què le darem que li sàpiga bo?*
*Què li darem al Fillet de Maria?*
*Què li darem al formòs Infantó?*

My nose is leaking from the cold; my eyes are leaking from the warmth. My heart must be leaking from fear. *What am I to do, Lord? What do I have to offer this child?*
The gift of trying? A desire to love? Is steadfastness in love enough?

# 49

## *Old Befana*

The more you get around from one season of time to the next the more you start to pick up on some sturdy threads that connect them. There are some that seem coarse, well-worn through the ages and they're not as attractive but they're unbreakable. The ones that are shimmering, delicate and alluring can break very easily and you find yourself lost with only the idea of the lovely thread to hang on to. And then there are the tangled ones and while they might look intriguing, those are the ones to be careful of, you need help with those.

Renae and her husband Gerome were kindhearted old folks in Pas-de-Calais; I'd know them both since they were small children and shared their fondness for all things sweet. They had grown up as best friends and then married when they were of age. They lived during such troubled times, though, poor folks. So many conflicts everywhere you looked. There were even contests to see who loved Jesus the right way. Attacks came from many sides between his own followers. New versions of his truths seemed to sprout up and twist things and then there were others who risked everything to stop the twisting. To top it all off there were rivals that began to fight against all of Jesus' followers. What a mess. Everywhere you looked people were getting upset and confused. Then the big bully unbelievers tried to swoop in and mop up the mess by stamping out belief altogether. But

Renae and Gerome were pretty unshakeable. They knew what they believed and they had their feet firmly planted in rich soil and their beliefs weren't going anywhere - especially when it came to Christmas!

They always made such a fuss about the birth of Jesus Christ. Oh how they'd work themselves into such a state. For eleven months of the year they were rather tranquil people who steadily worked in their vineyards or bottling their wines, but along the way they were putting away the best wines, the best fruits, the choicest meats and cheeses for the last month of the year. When the Advent season came along you would think that the success of the Christ child's birth depended on them alone. It was their self-appointed duty to bring everyone from town into their home on Christmas Eve and host a most commemorative feast in honor of the Holy Night. There was a definite spirit that moved them. It was an awful lot of work but each year they would arrange for musicians and vocalists to delight the guests with their various talents - the violinists playing *Jesu Joy of Man's Desiring* could make an old wooden statue like me melt like wax; the many flowers brought in from the greenhouses adorned the house with color and vibrancy; the crèche was the focal point of the feast - they added to it every year and included many different animals and characters: shepherds, innkeepers, and even a few Roman soldiers. It was magnificent!

While battles were being fought on fields, in courts and in castles, Renae and Gerome took no notice of all the squabbles against the faith and continued to live God's dream as they always had. For several weeks before the event the pair of them would prepare many foods for the Réveillon, particularly the Buche de Noel filled with the richest buttercream, which was everyone's favorite. Together, the townspeople, led by these gentle folks, would process to the Church of San Pierre and attend Midnight Mass together where something special happened as it did at every Mass – *he was there!* Oh yes, you could feel the presence of our God during that holy celebration; he was there in every way. The people would be filled with joy and after Mass they would run like the wind back to the house to give thanks and enjoy the wonderfully prepared dishes. I believe this is where the term *joie de vivre* came to be.

There were some townsfolk who scoffed at all the spiritual nonsense and preferred to carouse in their own fashion. They indulged in revelry without a reason which seemed to give them cause enough to celebrate in such manner whenever they felt the urge. But the Réveillon became a well-guarded tradition that attracted many people from nearby towns. When Renae and Gerome died, their son Michele sold the vineyards and the house, took the money and sailed off to distant lands. The townspeople felt marooned without their beloved Renae and Gerome to engage them in the communal affair. Some people went off to find other parties, but it wasn't the same and they felt sad even while reveling. Others joined the battles between faiths and still others abandoned the faith altogether. One day, André, the young man who had worked for Renae and Gerome on the vineyards for many years suggested that the feast never belonged to the old couple, it belonged to the purpose behind it. He put up a banner in town, *"Réveillon pour Jesu."* So, the townspeople pulled themselves together and carried on the tradition exactly as *le duo de Noël* had done before them. By golly, the sturdy thread continues to this very day!

Here, the child Nolly seems mildly aware of the fretfulness around her. She is helping Margaret decorate the house while Ivy is busy cleaning, and she helps Ivy prepare special treats when the mistress has business to tend to. It is clear to me anyway, that Ivy and Margaret are not working together. They are both intent on making certain that the child is able to have a memorable Christmas, perhaps her first memorable

Christmas as Margaret sees it, and perhaps her only one, as Ivy fears. There are traditions that each of them recall from happier times but their good intentions seem hollow without the bonds of love to hold the joy together. It is like they are going through the motions without remembering the purpose behind those motions. Pulling together a celebration for the sake of a child is a noble cause worth pursuing, and they are doing the best they can but they cannot seem to recover from their own disappointment in one another and they've lost sight of the spirit of the season. Ivy is hurt because she did not wish to choose between her employer whom she loves and her darling niece. Margaret is hurt because she is losing *Ivy*, the steadfast, unruffled servant who has been an anchor for her through her darkest moments; she has always kept the ship afloat, so to speak. She has relied on Ivy for so much, especially during this time of year. Ivy helped her to overlook this holiday altogether. Now, however, Ivy is unsteadied by her concerns for her future and Margaret is unsettled by an onslaught of repressed emotions. Both women cannot bear to recall the joy that Christmas used to bring before that Christmas that brought sorrow in this household, for it was on Christmas Eve two years ago, that little Joseph had died.

# 50

## *Margaret*

At first it was the wheezing sounds coming from his chest; then he could no longer open his beautiful blue eyes wide as he once had and he developed a darkening of the skin beneath them. The fever was relentless and the poor child suffered such pain in his chest and back – he could never lie comfortably – all of his little bones seem to ache without any relief. My darling little Joseph, how he'd suffered. I tried to hold him in my arms as much as possible. I looked to David for help but he seemed to need to be embraced as well. The doctors had called it neuroblastoma. There was nothing they could do. From the onset of his first symptoms until his final days, time was a painful blur, like an excruciating accident unraveling in slow motion.

His picture sits by my bedside table, the only portrait I have of him. Once he became ill, I did not want to remember him like that so there were no more pictures taken, no more games were played, no more celebrations and no more laughter. His beautiful life dissolved before our very eyes. At the end he seemed resigned and unafraid. He did not seem to fear an absence of life for he understood so little about being alive; rather he seemed concerned about us. Even with all his pain he was still just a child whose fulfillment came from making his parents smile. Learning to clap had made us smile; taking his first steps had brought us joy; uttering his first words made us celebrate but suddenly our worlds were turned upside-down and on some level *he knew*, he knew our sadness, our tears, our broken dreams were because of him and he still wanted nothing more from life than to make us smile. It was his only wish, and my poor little Joseph left this life with the feeling that he could no longer bring a smile to his Mommy and Daddy's hearts.

If Nolly's innocent understanding of heaven is to be believed, then Joseph knows there is no comfy place for him in my thoughts or in my heart; he sees that even after all this time since his pain ended only sadness lives in the place where the joy of him once lived. I have spent this time of year in this house to be near him. My sorrow is tied to his final suffering. Here, we are together. To remember him is to cry and to be filled with pain. I hug his picture to my heart. *My sweet boy, your life was meant to bring me joy not permanent sorrow.* The gates of my reserve have lately been weakened and long overdue sobs break through. *How can I let go? How can I possibly do what you're asking? How can I feel joy when I remember you? How can I invite you into my broken heart – how will it ever be a comfy place again?* I fall from my bed to the floor and bury my face in the rug, trying to muffle the sounds of my sobs but they refuse to be silenced. *Can it be that crying is the only way to commemorate your life? What a disservice I am doing to your memory. Tell me, Joseph, tell me my son, how can I smile again? You needed something from me then that I was powerless to give you, and you need something from me now that I feel unable to bring about. I have worn my sadness for you like a cloak to hold us both inside. I have offered more of my heart to the loss of you than to the love of you. Has love died with you? Should any mother feel joy again?*

Aunt Bess comes to mind. She had suffered such grief how many times? "My little loves died inside of me...." She'd warned me, "Don't give up on happiness... Don't leave here with the intention of remaining closed." Closed? Closed to what? I seem to lack the courage to open myself up to the unknown. "When you see that chance to heal, grab it!" I don't know how to heal. *I know I can't heal myself, Lord.* I sent David away, for together the burden of our pain was twice as heavy, but carrying it alone has not lightened my load at all. *What can I do?* I look into Joseph's face in the picture again. His smile is frozen in time. "Heaven is not a faraway place." *You are near, my baby. You are near.* I watched my baby suffer and die. I am not the first, nor shall I be the last mother to suffer in such a way. Love continues beyond death; a mother continues to be a mother even if her child is in heaven. She must open her arms wider to hold him, not close them in front of her. The comfy place within my heart must be a happy place for you to rest, little Joseph. *Forgive me, my little boy. Please, I need your forgiveness. Heaven help me. Dear God, I've been so broken and sad... can I ever find joy or peace again? Can I?*

# 51

## *Ivy*

Mrs. Livingston and I recall enough about past Christmas holidays, *happier Christmas holidays*, to know what to do to bring one about, at least on the surface. There must be plenty of festive décor, there must be cheerful music, there must be delicious foods in abundance, we must find a place to worship God, and of course a few gifts add an element of magic to the celebration. With only one more week until we produce a memorable Christmas for Nolly, I know for my part that I am revisiting past holidays and traditions that may be meaningful to my little darling. As a gift I am making a special book for her. Oh how she loves books. I am not a writer, nor do I have the time to sit and write a single word but I have little mementos that I am pasting into a blank journal. I can tell her the stories behind each memento and then she can recite them as she is so fond of doing.

The first page contains the one and only picture I have of our old home in Ireland. A passing caravan one day stopped by our farm and begged for some rashers of pork. Pa gave them plenty enough to take with them on the road. In gratitude, the man with the camera had taken our picture in front of our cottage. There is Pa and Ma standing straight and stern in the center. Their faces were too unfamiliar with photography to know what to do; they simply stared as if entranced and bewildered. Killian is standing next to Pa, smiling broadly beneath his dark cap and holding Archie the pig. Tim and Aidan are just in front of Killian, both wearing mischievous grins, probably because they are thinking of a prank to play on the family in the caravan. I'm standing next to Ma, holding Colleen in my arms, she is just a babe. This picture is all that remains of our family – until now. Nolly and I must carry on for the sake of these loved ones. She must be taught to know them and to love them. In time she will learn to love them as much as I did and together we will honor their memory.

I've added a few holy cards to the book because I know how much Nolly loves to tell stories about the saints. She has quite the imagination. She once told me that St. Patrick not only chased the snakes out of Ireland but he put them on a boat for America. He was afraid they would come back so he told the captain of the ship to take them to the far side of America. "What do you know about America?" I'd asked her. "I know I'd like to go there some day, but not where the snakes are. I heard about America in the house where Mommy and I stayed when you came to get us. People were talking about going there because they said America has lots of everything. It's even bigger than this house! But mostly, it has lots of growing space. That's what they said. Lots of growing space."

"Do you know what that means, Nolly? Lots of growing space?"

She'd put her finger on her chin and said, "I think it means there's lots of space for nice people to be nicer and lots of good things to make more good things. And lots of children and room to play and get bigger."

The things she says.

In the next few pages I have added some small treasures I'd found in Colleen's bag: a lock of Nolly's hair and a lock of Colleen's, a clipping of the bans in St. Finian's bulletin announcing Colleen and Danny Doyle's marriage. The remaining blank pages Nolly can fill with her own mementos. There is growing space in her little book.

# 52

## Margaret

The abandoned correspondence continues to sit beneath journals and layers of the *London Times* like relics from someone else's life. It's taken me a while to muster up the desire to sort through the mail. There was plenty of business that needed to be taken care of first. Ivy had diligently sent me anything that appeared urgent since I departed last spring but what remains on the blotter has not required my immediate, nor my gradual attention for that matter. I flipped through the statements from the bank, carefully placed on top and then saw once again the brown letter, judiciously placed at the bottom of the pile, which I've successfully ignored until now. Ivy is intuitive; she knows I do not wish to receive such letters but she's not so bold as to return them to sender without my instructions. Tapping my finger on the brown envelope, I vacillate between throwing it into the bin unopened, returning it like all the others, or, for heaven's sake, reading it once and for all.

An intense jangle of chirping sparrows congregating outside my window is reason enough to delay my actions. There must be twenty, twenty-five birds in the horse chestnut tree in the yard near Nolly's latest "nest." They have gathered amicably on several of the branches and now seem to be singing a soothing melody – agreeably distracting me from the matter at hand. David had written my name in a softer penmanship than he had on letters from the past. Some of his previous correspondences were printed in large, bold, and demanding letters, while this script seems almost suppliant. Nevertheless, I hesitate to read it. I am tempted once again to toss the letter into the bin and go about opening the bank statements and correspondences from some new business contacts. The sparrows have departed, there is silence, and my attention is drawn to the remaining leaves on the trees whose lively golden color has now faded to a dull brown. The departure of autumns' vibrancy has a tranquil effect and my heart once yearning for the stillness of winter now relishes the buoyant sound of birds. For a moment my head drops down into the emptiness beside me almost wishing it could drop against a living person.

The letter is still on the desk. I lift it and with the very tips of my fingers hold it above the bin for a moment or two. Why is David being so persistent? Why has this man not honored my wishes to be left alone? What does he want from me? I suppose there is only one way to find out. Margaret, I tell myself, read the letter.

I've opened it yet in my memory I see him walking toward the street away from the house with his green and blue carpetbag in hand… "I need you to leave here, David," I'd told him. "I cannot go on like this, as we have been. Please go and let me get through this." He'd been reluctant to go, insisting that I could go on, that life goes on. I was furious with him for relying on me to do the impossible. The letter beckons and I finally consent to read it.

*My dearest wife,*

*First and foremost what I wish to say is that I am deeply sorry. I cannot find words that will sufficiently express my regret for how I have failed you as a husband. I must say that I am grateful that you chose to return all of my previous unopened letters, and asked that the magistrate prevented me from coming to the house. This is not sarcasm; it is a genuine expression of understanding that* you were just and true to decline my pleadings to be readmitted back into your life. As I opened and reread the letters I had written I am ashamed and I am glad you did not read them. They were filled with childish pleas and rants as though your heart could endure those as well. I spent hours and hours crafting plausible explanations for my behavior and made demands that I had no right to make. I was wrong to have presumed so much about you, about us, and about our married life together. I genuinely apologize for being so closed off to your emotions and needs. It was my grave mistake to have presumed that we could pick up and continue on as we had before, to attend functions that could distract us from having to talk about or face our difficulties. I wanted my mode of life to remain unchanged and this was an unrealistic expectation. I never listened to you. I never tried to understand anything beyond my own needs and my own assertion about what was right for both of us.

My dearest Margaret, I ask, no, I beg your forgiveness. You bore the brunt of our marriage and our difficulties and sorrows alone because I refused to venture more intimately into our union. Was I frightened? I am being completely honest when I say that I was terrified. I have loved you with every ounce of my being since the moment I laid eyes on you. When you finally accepted my proposal I was shaken to the core. I wanted to be married to you, but I had no inkling about how to merit your love for me, nor did I know how to properly rise to the occasion of your deepest needs. You needed to share so much of yourself with me, more than I was willing to accept. I thought love was limited to feeling joy but it is wrong to limit love in such a way. I was inadequate at dealing with the loss of our beloved son and I was wrong and selfish to behave as though his loss had come between us. I should have worked harder to understand and share our mutual grief. I should never have doubted your love for me. As things became more difficult I struggled even harder against you and ventured further into my idea of what life should be. You bore so much on your own and you were justified when you asked me to leave you to yourself for you had already learned how to manage without my help. I believe that when all was said and done, my presence in your life must have seemed like a tremendous weight rather than a shoulder upon which you could *lean and be lightened in your sorrows. When you tried to speak to me I was not listening; I was busy trying to prepare my defense and justifications for why I was right. And this must have left you feeling entirely bereft of a husband. To face life each day without my constant bleating must have come as a relief. Oh, how I regret my inadequacy. I make no excuses about my deplorable weakness; I did not rely on the two of us together fostering the strength that we would both need.*

*Margaret, my dearest wife, I love you to this day. Should you wish to remain completely alone, I promise to honor your wishes from this moment forward. You have not filed for divorce, nor have you given me any reason to believe that you still wish to be married. I must confess, I have not resumed the lifestyle that I once longed for, for without you it all means nothing and I do not wish to resume living such a counterfeit life any longer. I never listened to what you wanted from life or what you needed from me. There has been no one else for me, not since I first saw you, and certainly not since we've separated. My darling, what I ask for now is not what I asked for in the past. I do not wish to be accepted back into your life so that we can pick up where we left off. I do not want that anymore. I want us. Marriage is not about you or me, it's about us. I want to devote myself to us as Margaret and David – us as a couple united in one heart. I will surrender myself to marriage and listen carefully to your heart as I never have before. If you wish to leave the city, the social life, the trappings of money and cultural expectations, just say the word. We can go away, live at Grange, or even take up a cottage in the Lake District, somewhere near Grasmere? I know how much you love it there and of course I share your love for Wordsworth. He was enamored with the serenity of the gentle hills and meadows and I can see the two of us building a harmonious life in such a place.*

*If you have read this letter to this point, I am grateful, my angel. I know from my solicitor that you have gone away and I hope you read this when you return. This will be my final letter and this is what I propose. If there is any measure of love that remains in your heart and you believe we can begin again, I ask only that we meet and begin to talk again. I make no demands. I wish only to have the opportunity to listen to what you were trying to tell me for so long.*

*So, my dear Margaret, I can only ask for a meeting. Should this meeting be welcomed I pray for more chances to listen to you. I would spend the rest of my life joining my heart to yours. If, however, you do not wish to meet with me, I will understand. If it is your wish I will take myself away from London and leave you in the peace you so greatly desire. I will not annoy you any further with pleas to see you and talk to you; I will go quietly away and live my life in solitude as well. I beg your forgiveness and your consideration to help me understand the way to live the life God meant for us as man and wife.*
*Yours forever,*

*David*

# 53

## *Old Befana*

I wish I had been able to catch up with those travelers and the wise men when they found the newborn king. There isn't a day that goes by that I don't imagine what that must have been like, to witness such a miracle. I can't say I haven't been lucky enough to see my fair share of miracles, but that one must have been astonishing. Can you imagine seeing God in the face of a small child? But, that's what this whole adventure has taught me, exactly that – to see God in all of his children. It sure makes a difference in how I can see things now than how I used to! It's the searching that has taught me to love him. No wonder he came as a child; you see, when we look into the beautiful face of an infant, we fall in love. We can actually feel our own love for God himself when we look at the baby! It wasn't until much later that I understood something else, something that I didn't see at the beginning. It wasn't until that child grew up, showed himself to be the Son of a caring God, all the things he did to show that he cares about *everything* that happens to us, that I began to understand. It was all tied up in what had happened to him and the way he died on that cross, and that's when I finally saw something new. It was the face that Pietro had carved into the wood; it was *that* face that revealed God's love for *us*. That's what Pietro understood: that this God of ours will go to any extreme to show us how much he cares about us and how much he wants us. I was alone before; I have never felt alone since I felt his love.

Oh, now listen to me carrying on like this; I can't help it, this Christmas season gets me all mushy and sentimental every single time. I'm so glad that I can be a part of this. Christmas isn't about me at all or those other characters that come around and bring a gift or two; it's about the caring God and how far he'll go to show us how much he loves us, no matter what bad things happen. It makes me want to do anything I can for him. It is that kind of love that drives people to do good things.

One Christmas I found myself with a family living on an island off the Atlantic coast. Such a nice family; they had three sons and a daughter. One of the sons had found me on his travels. The daughter was just the sweetest girl, beautiful in so many ways and quite cherished by her three older brothers. The brother I belonged to, Stan, always kept me in his pocket, just like Nolly does now. He said I brought him the luck he needed. Stan, his father, and his brothers were sailors; they made regular voyages to the mainland to buy supplies and medicines for the island. One of the things I liked the best about them was that their job was more than just a job to them, it was an opportunity to do something good. They made their regular trips to buy supplies and then return to sell them – that was the job they got paid to do. But often, and especially at Christmas, they went the extra nautical mile. They would return to the island with food and gifts and they gave them out to the islanders for free. They would even throw in a few trinkets for the families that had children.

On this one particular Christmas the sailors were quite troubled because there was a severe storm raging at sea and it was too dangerous to take a trip to the mainland and gather supplies (and gifts) before Christmas. The islanders assured them that Christmas could be celebrated when the seas became calm again; but as it happened, on Christmas Eve, a distress signal came from a small ship not far from the coast. The ship that had been caught up in the storm and was in danger of sinking. The family of sailors, along with three other volunteers from town, gathered in a meeting to decide on a course of action. They quickly discussed their plans to sail out to the distressed ship and help the passengers and crew. It would be dangerous, but all the men decided they could not bear the idea of sitting in their homes doing nothing while the cries from the ship could be heard shouting for help. The boat was dispatched and immediately the men knew that this treacherous storm was more powerful than their ability to navigate through its violent waters. After a couple of terrifying hours of bailing water out of the boat and trying to stay afloat, they reached the sinking ship. By the time they arrived, there were only about six passengers and one crew member remaining, hanging on to the mast.

Trying to help the terrified victims was a harrowing task. There were four children and two adults clinging to the remains of the ship. The men tried to help the children first. Stan, his brothers and two of the volunteers dove into the raging waters and grabbed the children one by one, struggling against vicious gale force winds and gigantic rogue waves. The children were lifted on to the boat; Stan's father fell into the waters while pulling a screaming child onboard. The brothers and their friends tried to save him but were pulled under by the current. In the end it was only Stan and one of the volunteers who made it back onto the boat with the children. They sailed back to the island with as much difficulty as they had sailed out. The islanders were crushed to see that the sailor, two of his sons, and two of the volunteers did not return. They had, however, returned with four trembling children who'd been captured from the West Coast of Africa and were headed to a different island in the Caribbean to be sold.

The sailor's wife was heartbroken to learn that her husband and two of her sons had perished at sea, a possibility she had always known had existed but she looked into the piteous eyes of these dark children who now had no parents and were as far from home as they could get and she actually blessed God for the unexpected opportunity to give them a home which is what she did. She, her daughter, and my Stan raised the four children, two girls and two boys as members of their own family. This wasn't an easy Christmas, but it was a valuable one. The young wife of one of the lost volunteers lamented the entire ordeal. They should never have gone out to save these people. Who were they anyway? It wasn't fair that such a horrible thing should happen to people who were trying to do something good. It would have been too bad, of course, if the children had died, but what was their life worth, considering their ultimate destination; they were going to be sold anyway. Why did such things have to happen to good people?

The truth of the matter, as I've learned it over the years, is that if bad things only happened to bad people the world would devour itself very quickly. I, for one, know that bad things happen to everyone but I think it's through the "good" people that we know God is with us and helping us. When something good comes from evil it is the kiss of God's grace upon the world. I see how strongly he cares about everything that happens. Fear and hurt are changed into an inspirational light instead of tragedy buried in irrevocably bad circumstances. Put an ailing plant into fertile soil and you cultivate beauty and abundance. Put the ailing plant into barren dust, and that's the end of that. It's all about salvaging the good in a mess of bad. It's a pretty decent goal if you ask me.

# 54

## *Ivy*

A savory beef in provincial wine sauce has been prepared as my mistress prefers it. Though at the time when many family members surrounded the table in the dining room on Christmas Eve, a turkey or goose was the favorite choice. Now, says the mistress, a goose it is far too much trouble for the two and a half ladies that will feast on this solemn night. She insisted that in addition to her favorite beef, I prepare a favorite dish of my own and Nolly's so I have chosen my mother's recipe for diced potatoes with butter, onion, sage and parsley. Nolly suggested placing a red pepper in the potatoes to give it the "red and green" look of Christmas. "And don't forget the peas, Auntie, they are green, too!" When I asked her about her favorite Christmas dish so I can prepare it as well, she put her finger on her chin once again and frowned. "I can't remember," she said. Poor little thing. She probably can't remember a special Christmas dinner.

"Let me help you remember, then, Nolly," I advised. "Was it Irish Soda Bread?" She shook her head, no. "Was it candied carrots or turnips?" No, again. "How about Irish Christmas pudding?" Her eyes lit up like stars. "Oh yes, Auntie, that must be it!" So, together in the kitchen we labored to prepare the best Christmas pudding made with plenty of raisins, sugar, spices, butter and bread. I also added some Irish whiskey I'd purchased yesterday morning just for this occasion, but not too much; I never liked it when the pudding tasted more like a soused rag than a dessert.

When Nolly dipped her finger into the pudding mixture and tasted it on the tip of her tongue, she threw her arms around my waist and hugged me close. "Oh, Auntie, Christmas is wonderful. It will always be wonderful." Reminding me of our uncertain future together, I heaved a heavy sigh, and stirred the pudding with a bit more effort. This will be a memorable Christmas, indeed, but what lies ahead will most certainly be a trial. I will do my very best by this precious child. I suddenly had the urge to hold her in my arms. I let go of the pudding and picked Nolly up and held her close. She pushed her warm hands against my cheeks and said, "Auntie, God will bless you!" Where she comes up with these things, I do not know. It made me laugh and respond by saying, "I pray he does, child, but I pray even more that he blesses *you!*"

"He already has," she says, and wiggles to get down again.

## 55

## *Margaret*

I have carried David's letter in my pocket for three days and now, upstairs in my bedroom, I have tucked it away beneath my mother's embroidered handkerchiefs in the drawer next to my bed. I don't want Ivy to see it when she comes upstairs with my warm milk and peppermints. I have been very anxious and quite frankly at a loss to know what to do. David is right in one respect, I have not moved in any direction – neither to end our marriage, nor to reconcile it. For two years I have been acting as though ignoring it will make it go away. I have been vehemently avoiding any contact with him because I simply wanted to pretend that nothing ever happened – not the love, the joy, the excitement, the dreams, the wonder, the plans, nor the fear, the hurt, the devastation, the disappointment, or the defilement of a happy life. I tried to convince myself it was all just a dream. Some of it was happy, but the rest was a nightmare. The strangest part of my life in the last few years is that it is difficult to understand whether I have now been simply dreaming or completely benumbed by life.

"Here you are, Ma'am," Ivy says as she walks into my room with a tray of warm milk but instead of my usual peppermints there is a small cookie that Nolly sent up to the Missus for Christmas Eve and for "sweet dreams."

"Thank you, Ivy. Tell Nolly thank you, as well. She is very considerate."

"She is very happy, Ma'am. Tonight was lovely. I know how difficult this is for you but I honestly don't think she will ever forget this. She enjoyed the piano and the stories very much. I can't believe she stayed awake through Midnight Mass. She was so enthralled! Thank you, Ma'am, for allowing both of us to share in a special celebration with you tonight. I don't know if Nolly will not sleep a wink tonight. She is quite enchanted by the idea of spending Christmas day with you. You have been so kind to her, Ma'am, spending time with her, playing music at the piano, reading to her, and listening to the endless stories she invents. I thank you. Your kindness has meant the world to both of us."

"She is a special, child, Ivy. She has been more of a pleasure than I expected."

"Yes, Ma'am. She certainly is. Good-night, then."

Though Ivy leaves the room, I feel her continued presence, and Nolly's, and tonight I sense David's as well. It is like there is a room full of people here with me, demanding that my thoughts give them the attention they are due. Joseph is here as well, perhaps it is his presence that demands the most from me. What does a dead child need from his mother? I put my hands up to my face to hide my shame but I cannot hold back the tears. *Tell me Joseph, I'm listening, what do you want from me?*

## 56

## *Old Befana*

My favorite day of the year! The Christmas punch is being served. There is a savory beef and potatoes, peas, Christmas pudding and some heavenly apple tarts that Margaret ordered from the bakery. Margaret promises there is one more surprise which seems to make Nolly almost convulse with excitement. The branches of the Christmas tree seem to be even perkier today, showing off their decorations and splendor. There are twelve red candles on the table – one for each day of Christmas. The poinsettia flowers are arranged in a row toward the unused end of the long table so it won't seem so obvious that there are so many empty places. Nolly was permitted to sprinkle a bit of hay between each plant to remind them that the Baby Jesus was born in a stable, and if that weren't enough she even abducted the small figurine of Christ from his place in the crèche to be invited to the table where his place of honor is at the very center.

When the three ladies sit down together at the table, it is the child who reminds them to thank the Baby Jesus for letting them have his birthday dinner together. Margaret and Ivy exchange smiles and bow their heads.

"In the name of the Father, and of His Son, and of His Holy Spirit," begins the child. "Thank you, Baby Jesus, for giving me the best Auntie and the best Missus. I feel like I have a family. Thank you for letting me have a birthday tomorrow! I'm going to be five. We almost have one together! Thank you that the Missus is so nice, and that my Auntie makes us happy. And thank you for granny who knows what we need. And thank you for Mommy in heaven who still needs me to be good. And thank you... umm, thank you for all the things I forget. Amen."

At first they ate in silence. Ivy felt awkward eating at the family table for the first time ever. Nolly, though usually very chatty while eating, seemed to be thinking about what comes next after a Christmas meal. Margaret, for her part, spent less time eating and more time watching her dinner companions.

"Is it not to your liking, Ma'am?" Ivy asked her. "If you'd like I can certainly prepare another dish for you."

"Ivy, this is the best Christmas dinner I have ever had the pleasure to enjoy. You have outdone yourself in so many ways. Nolly is right, you make us happy. Nolly, Auntie Ivy recently told me that it is your birthday tomorrow, but I thought it was fitting that we should enjoy a birthday surprise today and carry over the celebration into tomorrow as well. Would you like that?"

"Oh, Missus!" That was all she could say for the excitement was too much for her. She ran out of the dining room and could be heard losing her Christmas dinner into the waste bin in the kitchen. Both Margaret and Ivy dashed out of their seats to follow her. It was Margaret who lifted the child when she was finished heaving. Ivy wiped the child's mouth. At the same time, they both asked Nolly if she was okay.

Nolly's eyes were glossy from being sick; she covered her mouth and said, "I forgot to thank the Baby Jesus for the food."

Margaret smiled. "It's never too late to say thank you, Nolly. Come now; let's rest in the study, shall we? Perhaps all the excitement was too much. I will read you the Christmas story again." Turning to Ivy she said, "Leave the dishes until later. Come and join us in the study."

"I will be in shortly, Ma'am. I'll just put the food away."

"Long ago, in a land far, far away, there was a young woman named Mary who was married to a kind man name Joseph..." Margaret began to read. Nolly seemed to feel much better now and much calmer than she had during dinner. She sat in the nook of Margaret's arm and listened quietly to the story, unlike the night before when she'd felt the need to add further details that the author had somehow overlooked. Ivy came into the room and sat in the seat nearest the tree. She saw that there were two more gifts that she had not seen the day before. She had added her own before going to bed and wondered at the wrapping of some of the gifts that seemed so incongruent – two small paper sacks tied with old ribbon. It must be Nolly's doing.

A deeply peaceful feeling washed over Margaret today. When she finished reading, she asked Nolly if she thought she felt well enough to open a gift or two. Nolly nodded her head and sat up straight with her hands folded in her lap. She looked like she was expecting the Baby Jesus himself to present the gifts.

"Ivy, I see you are sitting near a few packages. Perhaps you can give Nolly what you have for her."

"Me, Ma'am? I thought you might wish to go first." Margaret simply shook her head.

Ivy handed Nolly the little book she'd made and for the next few minutes explained the meaning behind each memento inside. Nolly kept running her finger over the locks of hair that had been tied to the pages. She commented on how different her hair was from her Mommy's. Margaret's eyes glistened when she saw how tenderly the child was affected by these small treasures.

Next, Ivy handed Margaret a gift. It was a new mug with a Celtic symbol of friendship painted in red, and a box of peppermints. The note attached said, "May you always find comfort before you sleep. Love, Ivy." Margaret understood – soon she would not have Ivy to bring her these special succors at night when going to bed. She nodded her head and thanked Ivy with a soft tone in her voice. "I do not believe we should make Nolly wait any longer. Would you like to give your gifts Nolly?" Nolly nodded and went for the brown paper packages under the tree. First, she gave her gift to her auntie. Ivy unwrapped the gift. It was a little star which had been assembled with twigs and tied together with yellow ribbons. Nolly said, "Auntie, this is a Christmas star and it will bring you something special." Ivy reached over and pulled Nolly close and kissed her. "It worked," she said. "It brought me you!" Nolly clapped her hands in delight. Then she turned to Margaret and handed her a gift and said, "For you, Missus."

"Why, Nolly, dearest, I didn't expect to receive a gift. Thank you!"

"Open it," said Nolly.

Margaret carefully pulled off the brown paper and gently lifted an unusual ornament of sorts. It seemed to be a heart made of two pieces and tied together with more yellow ribbons. "Nolly, this is lovely," she said.

"Missus, I made it for you. See, these are wings."

"I don't understand," said Margaret.

"I had an angel that my Mommy gave me when we lived at that other house with lots of people. On the way here to your house I dropped my bag and she broke. I couldn't fix the angel part. Mommy was sick so she couldn't fix her either. But she took the two angel wings and showed me that when you put two angel wings together it makes a heart. So the important part doesn't have to be broken anymore."

Margaret exchanged a look with Ivy. "Your niece is truly remarkable, Ivy." Ivy smiled in agreement. "Come here, Nolly. May I give you a hug? I know you're not my niece but you feel like you could be." Nolly laughed and joyfully initiated the embrace herself.

"Well, now I would like to give each of you my gifts," said Margaret. "Ivy, this is for you, and Nolly, I put yours in the hall cupboard. I will go and get it." Ivy opened her gift and found the Irish music box. She ran her finger over the engraving then opened it to hear the tune. It was her special song that reminded her of home. Nolly peered inside to see what was making the music and saw nothing. "It's like magic," she said and clapped her hands at the wonderful little box filled with enchantment.

Margaret came into the room carrying a large parcel wrapped in copious amounts of festive paper. Nolly stood and watched her enter the room, not believing for one minute that something so huge could be her special gift. Her widened eyes reflected all the flickering candlelight from the Christmas tree. She dare not hope something so big could be for her.

Margaret set the parcel down on the floor and said, "Merry Christmas, Nolly. This is for you."
Immediately, Nolly's hands went to her cheeks and she looked up at Margaret with disbelief. "Well, open it!" Margaret said.

Nolly sat on the floor and tried to untie the ribbon. Ivy and Margaret sat down on the floor beside her and helped her to pull off the ribbon and wrapping. It was the dollhouse Nolly had seen in the attic! Nolly looked at it in such wonderment and surprise. "This is for me?" she asked.

"Yes, Nolly, this is for you. I have been sorting through quite a number of things in this house to decide what to take with me to Grange and what to leave behind. When I came across this dollhouse I knew it needed you. It has been alone and unoccupied for far too long. It needs a loving child. I know how much you love to make little homes, comfy places, and I thought you might enjoy this. I played with it all the time as a child. My mother used to sit and play with me, too. My sisters preferred other toys, but this was always my very favorite – a home. I have no child to give it to, but I want to give it to you."

"Thank you, Missus," Nolly said quietly.

"Look, here in the box there is more furniture, and a family. You can decorate it and put the family in there if you'd like. I hope you will enjoy it as much as I did."

"I like it very much, Missus. Thank you. I will take care of the family."

"I know you will, my dear."

Nolly was enthralled with the dollhouse. Before arranging the furniture or handling the family, she simply wanted to run her hands over every inch of its ornately decorated roof, windows of different shapes, gingerbread trimmings, the porch, the doors, the chimney – everything. It was as if she were trying to make sure it was real and not just a wonderful dream.

"There is one more thing I should like to ask you both," Margaret said. She fidgeted with her hands and her breath trembled as she spoke. "Tomorrow is St. Stephen's day, and Nolly it is your birthday. I would like celebrate your birthday Nolly, all of us together – a meal at the Seymour's hotel. That was my surprise! I do not wish for you, Ivy, to labor over yet another feast! I would very much like for all of us to…" She let the sentence drop; her throat would not let one more word pass through.

"Yes, Missus. Yes, Ma'am." Both Ivy and Nolly replied in unison. Nolly clapped her hands again. Margaret recovered and nodded hesitantly. "In the morning, I will have a visitor… uh, Mr. Livingston, my husband, will be stopping by to talk and then we can go to have a marvelous lunch." Nolly was delighted and then became reabsorbed in her dollhouse. Margaret felt overwhelmed with emotion. She rose and walked over to the window. She carried the heart that Nolly had given her. Ivy approached her. "Ma'am, is there anything I can get you? Tea? Or anything I can do to help you tomorrow?" Margaret shook her head.

"Ivy, do you believe that two people rise above the detritus of life?"

"It's my understanding, Ma'am, that love is all that matters. It can rise above anything."

"You have been with me through it all, the joys and the sorrows. You've been by my side more than my own sisters and stood by with such quiet strength, carrying on with such dedication."

"Everything will be all right, Ma'am," Ivy said gently.

"You said that to me once before. I did not believe in such platitudes, but you were sincere in your expression. It was your wish for me, not a banal assertion. Forgive me. I seem to be asking that a lot lately." Ivy' brows pinched together. She had no idea how to respond. Margaret looked away and fingered the heart that Nolly had given her. "Yes. Yes, a fresh start in a new place. At least it's a step. Stagnation has not served me well." She sighed. "How about some tea for all three of us?"

It isn't every day you get to see the colors of human hearts band together into a spectrum of light. This is why I always say giving life a chance is always better than the desperate, loveless way of doing things. The spirit of this wonderful, caring God accomplishes such wonders. He works through every one of us. When I began this journey long ago I thought I was seeking a baby but what I've found along the way never ceases to amaze me. By golly if he isn't always with me. Love is a place to live not just a feeling or an idea. The Son of the caring God opened our eyes to such a place in which to dwell. He stretched out his arms and invited us all in like orphaned children. The night of the star was an open invitation to everyone, even a little old recluse like me. I'll tell you this much: living without the love of a caring God is not a place where I would want to live. I like the comfy place he's made for me. In this place there is no fear; it is whole and beautiful and a far cry from nothing. Christmas Day is a good reminder of all I've learned and this is one that I'm going to *remember*.

# 57

## *Kathy*

Moving to a new home after spending thirty-eight years in the same house must be like going into the hospital for a skin transplant. The new place, with all your belongings, is like the same you on the inside but it all feels different. The headache part of moving is the decision-making process: what to pack, what to give away, and what to throw away. The longer a family spends in a house, the more decisions there are to be made about such things. I know it's all just stuff, but it's the stuff of love. These are the expressions of love: all those little treasures we save along the way, the kids' special toys, their artwork that once hung on the fridge with colorful magnets, the threadbare blankies and stuffed animals require decisions that the heart may or may not be prepared to make. Francis isn't much help. If it were up to him he'd say, "Throw it all away" and if I objected he'd say "Pack it all up and bring it along." No decisions required. It's too much work to pack up things we don't need, it's heartbreaking to throw anything away, and my ability to make these decisions weakens as I go along with this task. These little treasures have somehow replaced the little people that once owned them. Our kids are grown now and on their own with their own families, and I've given many things to my grandchildren, but still... Francis believes that if we move to a smaller home requiring less maintenance we will be happier. I'm not unhappy. Well, I suppose I'm just feeling the breadth of that void left behind by years of intense mothering gone to the wayside. Never mind, Francis is right, staying here just reminds me of how fast our lives slip away. Before you know it, our children will be going through the things I decided to keep and figuring out whether to throw them away, give them away, or keep them. The cycle of life.

There is a box I seriously don't know what to do with and it is up to Francis to go through these things, whether he wants to or not.

"I haven't seen this stuff in years," he says, and slaps his thigh. "Holy baloney, look at this! It's the old catcher's mitt I kept at my grandmother's house. Look at this! This box is full of my grandmother's stuff! I can't believe we still have Grandma Nolly's things. There's an old scrapbook here with some locks of hair. She even added mine to this book. Oh, wow, Kathy, check this out!"

"What is it?" I asked. Then I take a closer look. "I remember that. Why she used to have that sitting on that table by the window. I remember there was a really old doily with some other antique knick-knacks on it. Let me see it."

It's a little figurine of an old woman. She is wearing a scarf around her head and carrying a broom in one hand and a sack on her back. It's funny, if you look at her one way she just looks old, wrinkly, and pensive. If you turn her another way, she is smiling like she's looking right at you.

"She used to tell us so many stories about that doll," Francis said.

"It's not a doll," I corrected him. "It's a priceless figurine. I say we definitely keep her. The grandkids would get a kick out of her. What were the stories she used to tell about this? The kiddies are coming over this afternoon to help us pack, I'm sure they'd love to hear them."

"Are you kidding me; they're coming to help? They're going to break stuff. I thought it was just Alison and Jay coming over; I didn't know they were bringing the kids, too."

"Don't worry. I'll assign them the 'give-away' stack to pack up. They'll be fine."

Francis is still staring at the little statue and lost in his memories. I notice that he is fingering his grandmother's old rosary. She was never without it. Now, he puts it into his pocket, not back in the box. He was so close to his grandmother and he's always been very open-hearted just like she was.

When the kids arrive, it is six year-old Jason that wanders into the room to sit with Francis and the old box. Jason is walking slowly because his bones are hurting again and he's been getting sick. Of course, he will go into the hospital again. Helping Grandpa to go through old treasures and pack them up is a good thing for him to do today before he starts up treatments again. He's captivated with the old woman statuette and listening to Francis tell his old tales.

"This little statue was my grandmother's most-loved treasure. It was one of the few things she brought with her from England when she was young and married my grandfather Frank. She said it meant the world to her."

"Where did she get it?" Jason asked.

"Hmm. My Grandma Nolly was an orphan. Her parents died when she was little. She went to live with her Aunt Ivy that worked as a housekeeper for a rich lady in London. That's where she got the statue – from the rich lady. My grandmother used to say that this little statue loves to travel around. That's why she always carries this knapsack on her back. She's been all over the world."

"Where did the rich lady get it?" Jason asked.

"I have no idea kiddo. My grandmother didn't say, but I'll tell ya, she used to talk a lot about those times. She said she had two moms and a dad. The rich lady decided to move north when she and her husband patched things up and they invited my grandmother and Ivy to go with them. They lived as a family. Things were a little rough during World War I, even for the rich folks. They sold off a lot of their business holdings but kept Ivy and my grandmother there at the house like family not servants. Eventually, they used their house as a home for kids that needed someplace to go during the war. They even brought in an elderly friend of the family, a "real granny," she called her. My Grandma Nolly said for someone who had no parents and siblings she ended up with more than her fair share of family. When my grandmother was twenty-one, she met my grandfather Frank. He was a soldier during the war. He said the thing he loved the most about grandma was the sparkle in her eyes. She had it as long as I knew her until the day she died. After grandma and grandpa got married they moved back here to Ohio where grandpa was from and that's how the statue ended up here. My grandmother used to call it granny."

"That's funny. Who's granny was she? What was her real name?"

"Grandma Nolly used to say that her real name was Befana. She started out in Italy, I guess. She acts like everyone's granny. She brings them little treats at Christmas time or, I guess after Christmas, on the day the three kings brought presents to Jesus."

"Why does she do that?"

"The story goes that she's looking for Baby Jesus. That's why she travels around and she leaves little treats just in case the child she finds is Jesus. My grandma loved this little statue all her life."

"Did it bring her treats?"

"It brought her a lot more than that. She said it brought her a brand new life. Grandma Nolly was a wise old thing."

"Nolly is a funny name, isn't it, granddad?"

"It's not common, that's for sure. Her name was actually Nollaig. She was born in Ireland. Nollaig is the Irish version of Noelle."

"Like my sister!" Jason exclaimed.

"That's right, kiddo. I think you and Noelle should keep this statue at your house now in a very special place. Can you do that?"

"Yes, granddad. At Christmas time will she bring us treats?"

"I suspect she'll bring you much more than that."

CPSIA information can be obtained at www.ICGtesting.com
Printed in the USA
LVOW03s0029211015

459008LV00003B/182/P